SOS HOTEL

FRIENDLY SANCTUARY FOR THE FIENDISHLY FABULOUS

SOS HOTEL

BOOK 2

ADAM VEX

BLURB

It's been two weeks since the SOS Hotel opened, and everything is going *great* . . .

Apart from the detective who's dead set on accusing Zee of murder, the leaking pipes, a psycho sorcerer stalker, a shadowbeast in the attic, and . . . did I mention Lord Reynard has a wife? Yeah, he didn't mention it either. I could have done with knowing that before, you know, kinda falling for the suave, sexy Vampire Daddy.

He also neglected to mention that his wife wants my head on a plate. Literally.
This is not the love triangle I was expecting.

If Reynard lied about that, what else is a lie? Is Zee right, and Lord Reynard wants our hotel? Or is it something more personal he desires, such as my heart?

My name is Adam Vex. I'm totally, one hundred percent human.

Welcome to the SOS Hotel.

Where it's about to get weird-*er*.

SOS Hotel is a whacky MMM adventure about a vampire lord, an ex-porn-star demon, and a boring human who absolutely does not have any *secrets. 18+ only. You'll find dark humor abounds, plus explicit language and sex. If you don't like the f-word, or sex, with a little mass murder thrown in, do not read these books.* **There will be triggering content for some, including sexual coercion.** *Proceed with caution.*

Have a great stay!

CHAPTER 1

THE CRAWL SPACE behind the hotel walls was barely wide enough to wriggle through, but as Claymore was still missing, someone had to fix the leaky pipe. We couldn't afford a plumber, so I'd picked up a wrench and some tape, and figured I'd fix it myself. It had seemed like a good idea at the time, but after a face full of cobwebs, and some unfortunate, tiny skeletons crunching under my shoes, I'd begun to rethink a few life choices.

The leak plink-plinked on the floorboard ahead. *Almost there . . .*

I knelt by the wet patch that had stained the ceiling in the room below, and eyed the dripping elbow joint. More tape, maybe?

A screeching gremlin dashed out of the dark—at my face.

They say gremlins are more afraid of us than we are of them, but whoever coined that phrase, didn't have one trying to claw their eyes out. I swung the wrench like a bat, and may have screamed . . . just a little. I'm not proud of it. What I am proud of, however, were the impressive contortionist maneuvers I pulled while escaping the eight-inch-wide space, prior to tumbling out the access panel.

The gremlin had scarpered, but I wasn't alone.

Blinking through the dust cloud, I looked up at the hotel's most impeccably dressed resident who, of course, chose that precise moment to appear.

"Adam." Lord Reynard said, peering down his nose, while I gazed up from the floor. "I heard a scream."

I coughed. "Ugh."

He offered his hand, which I naturally took. Mercy, he had soft skin. Did he moisturize? Some stories told of how vampires were virus-animated corpses, but I'd been close to Reynard a few times now, and he definitely was not cold, or stiff. Mostly, the opposite—warm, and reassuringly hard.

He hauled me to my feet. I stumbled into his impeccable, suit-clad chest. Dust rained off me and dared land on his black jacket. "Oh, sorry, you got a little—" I brushed a cobweb from his lapel and smeared a handprint there instead. "Oops."

"Adam, do please refrain from helping," he said, flicking at the jacket.

"Right." I coughed up more dust—or maybe that fresh cloud came from my hair—and moved away. "Were you uh passing, or . . . ?"

"As I said, I heard a scream." He plucked webs from his jacket, then raised his gaze. "Are you quite alright?"

"Yeah, it was just . . ." I planted my grubby hands on my hips, trying to act as though I hadn't just screamed like a damsel in distress. "We really need to do something about the gremlins."

"You screamed because of a gremlin?"

"It was really fast." I puffed. "Like, *so* fast, and it came *at* me." I mimed what I hoped looked like a gremlin launching at my face, but his meagerly arched eyebrow was not an impressed reaction. "You had to be there."

"Well, I see you're well, and my assistance is not required. I'll leave you to go about the rest of your day." He glided toward the door, polished black shoes barely making a sound on the soft carpet.

Had he rushed from wherever he'd been in the hotel because he'd heard my scream? I should probably apologize. "Erm . . . thank you?"

We'd met almost two weeks ago, when he'd decided to check in at the SOS Hotel. He'd been instrumental in helping to save Zee, my business partner, from a psychotic sorcerer posing as a real estate mogul, who was super grumpy about my buying the hotel out from under him. Yeah, it had been an interesting first few days.

Reynard had been absent since we'd saved Zee. I'd begun to wonder if we'd see him again, but here he was, looking as refined as ever. Silky smooth black hair flowed down his back, without a single strand out of place. And those silvery eyes—they never got any less tantalizing.

"You're welcome. Oh, and Adam? Are you busy this evening?" he asked, pausing at the door but keeping his back to me.

"Busy? I . . . erm . . . Well, there's always something to do around he—"

"Dinner. With me. My driver will collect us at eight." He was gone before I'd had a chance to agree. Or decline. Although, there hadn't been any chance of my saying no. Not really.

Dinner. With Lord Reynard. Vampire nobility. Well, that would be . . . nice.

But then I remembered our deal. In exchange for his help saving Zee, he got to suck on my veins. Friends with benefits. My only stipulation had been that he take me to dinner first.

So was this a prelude to that? Or was it an actual dinner, with no strings attached?

I looked down at my tattered clothes. I'd deliberately worn old jeans and a stained shirt, knowing I'd be crawling in the walls, but frankly, I resembled something the street sweepers had peeled off Demontown's asphalt on a Saturday morning.

Someone as polished as Reynard did not want to date this mess. I'd also been clear, when negotiating our deal, that it wasn't a date, but a mutually beneficial agreement. He got blood, and I got . . . hard, without the pay-off. But also, his help with saving Zee—so I owed him for that.

The dinner was a business arrangement, nothing more.

I left the room and marched down the corridor. I should have asked if it was black tie. It *had* to be black tie, didn't it? Reynard wore a suit for everything. He probably *slept* in a suit. I didn't even own a dinner jacket.

Could I hire a tux?

I'd spent every last cent on the hotel.

I'd have to borrow something, and the only person I knew who may have a tuxedo, was Zee. I found him in the lounge, draped across a large three-seater couch—wings out, tail trailing across the floor, horns gleaming. The too-tight crop top, stretched across his pecs, read: *Not Your Baby.*

He looked like a work of art. A splash of demonic sex appeal, that hadn't gone unnoticed by the rest of the guests—mostly the women, but some men too. They squealed and giggled in little groups, trying to take pictures on phones that didn't work very well within our wards.

I stared like the rest of them, and shook myself awake. *I* knew he was gorgeous. The *guests* knew he was gorgeous. *Everyone* knew he was gorgeous. He did not need to lounge around, advertising the fact. "Hey, Zee? Don't you have a room to sleep in?"

He cracked an eye open—far too alert to have been asleep. He'd been faking it, quietly soaking up the attention. "Shoo, I'm working here."

"Great, but you're a manager, not wall art. There are other important things to take care of, like the gremlins in the walls, the leaking pipes, the creaky elevator. And we still don't have a handyman." I puffed my bangs from my face.

He huffed, sat up, and planted his boots on the floor. His wings flicked out, like someone cracking their knuckles, and his fans across the room swooned. I got it. Zee was difficult *not* to admire. We'd recently crossed the business-partner boundaries and gotten real personal with each other, so I knew exactly how one glance from Zee could turn a man's blood to lava. But there was a place and time to absorb lust— at the bar, on his stage. Not in the hotel lounge.

He blinked his long-lashed purple eyes. "What's got your panties twisted?"

"I'm uh . . . I'm going out, and I need a suit, or a tuxedo. Something nice to wear."

"Going *out*?" He rose to his impressive height and stretched his arms, making the top ride up even further. A glorious display, of abs and a curvy waist, drew the eye down to his arrow tattoo.

"You never go out." He sauntered toward the bubbling group of fans, took the hand of one, and fluttered a kiss across the back of her knuckles. The young woman sounded as though she'd orgasmed right there. Her squeals followed us into the lobby.

"Business or pleasure, Kitten?" Zee asked.

The guests in the lobby all looked over, since nobody could *not* look at the package that was Zodiac. He added a sway to his hips, and left his wings hanging open, as though relaxed. His tail swished behind him, emphasizing each strut. It all seemed effortless, but every single step was designed for maximum ogling power, and I caught myself admiring the symphony of movement. His firm, hot body had quivered under my hands, and that tail had expertly jerked me off, while his cock had filled me up.

I tore my gaze away. It was supposed to be a one-time thing, because he'd been starving, but how could I forget it? Not to mention the prickly wall of tension that had appeared between us since that night. We probably just needed time . . .

We'd always worked well together, side by side, but since I'd helped *feed* him, he'd been keeping his distance—and to be honest, so had I. It was easier not to be around him now I knew how delicious *all that* tasted.

And how I craved tasting him again.

"Uh, business, I think," I said, barely remembering he'd asked a question.

"Business," he purred, entering the elevator. "Should I be there?"

"No, nope, I've got it." If I mentioned Reynard, he'd get sassy. Zee didn't trust him, but he also hadn't been conscious when Reynard had posted an online appeal to help save his life, so . . . since Reynard was leaving at the end of the month, it wasn't worth the drama.

The doors rumbled closed, and the elevator jolted into motion. We'd kissed in here. Or, more accurately, I'd thrown myself at him, and he'd kissed me back, until he'd decided I hadn't been in my right mind and didn't want him like that. I *had* been in my right mind. And I *did* want him. But it was complicated. "You know, you can't use this hotel like your own personal buffet," I grumbled.

"Excuse me?"

"We have the bar and the stage, and when you're performing, that's fine, but displaying yourself all over the place to be stared at by guests? I'm not sure it's right."

"I was *sleeping*, Kitten." He grinned, not even attempting to hide the lie.

"No you weren't, you were feeding. If people think you're just here to feed on them, they won't come."

"They might not come, but I will." He leaned against the side of the elevator and picked at his sharp nails. "Wait . . ." His eyes narrowed. "Are you jealous?"

"No." I folded my arms and watched the numbers count up. "That's not . . . No."

"Oh, Kitten. You fucking *are*." He pushed off the side and muscled into my personal space. His sharp nail poked into my chin as he tilted it up, so I had to look into his eyes. Eyes that held a thousand promises in their multifaceted depths. "But we aren't a thing, you and me. We made that clear."

"Exactly." I brushed his hand away. "Which is why I'm *not* jealous. You can't turn the hotel into Razorsedge, is what I'm saying."

His smile died, and he stepped back, wings closing.

The elevator arrived at his floor, and we strode wordlessly down the corridor. Perhaps I shouldn't have mentioned Razorsedge, the porn club where he'd been the headliner.

He swept inside his room, toward the wall of wardrobes, then flung open all the doors, displaying a rainbow of a hundred outfits. "They won't fit your . . . stats, but Madame Matase can adjust anything you like." He plucked a neon blue suit with silver buttons from the rail and held it against me, scrunching his face in thought.

"Uh, it's nice. But maybe something a bit more subtle?"

"So, the look you're going for is fucking dull?" He shoved the blue suit back and screeched the hangers along the rail. His tail lashed. He was definitely angry. I'd only told him the truth—he couldn't use the hotel as his own personal buffet. We had to be careful. These first few weeks would determine the hotel's future, and our reviews on Hotels4U weren't great so far—ignoring the sockpuppet ones that were so obviously Zee rating us five stars. I'd had to ask him to remove those.

In the corner of my eye, his tousled bed lay in wait, like an unspoken invite to jump in for round two and maybe shake out some of the electric tension sizzling between us. I couldn't be the only one noticing our vibe was off. Zee was attuned to emotions. He had to be feeling it too . . .

I feared we'd made the itch worse, instead of getting rid of it. Maybe *itch* was the wrong word, although, standing in the same room as him did have parts of me craving his touch. And it had nothing to do with his allure. This need to kiss every inch of his skin—all the way down his body, from the tip of his horns to the end of his tail—was all mine.

"Hold this." He shoved an outfit into my hands, that appeared to consist of multiple belts riveted together with steel studs. Where the, uh . . . male genitals went, a sling would cradle the most precious, dangling bits, in a snug leather pouch. "Here." He took the leather belt outfit back and shoved a tux into my hands instead. "Try that. Then come back and we'll do something about your hair."

"What's wrong with my hair?"

He winced, reached out, ruffled it, and plucked a cobweb free. "Has a gremlin been nesting in here?"

A zip of static jolted between us. He gasped, and stumbled against the cupboard door. I shivered, letting the pleasant little zap work its way through me.

"What the fuck was that?"

I shrugged. "Probably nothing."

He shook out his hand. "Right. *Nothing*. Except it felt a lot like the wards kicking in. I wasn't going to hurt you." He frowned at his hand, and shook it out again.

"I know." It hadn't felt like the wards to me. I was still feeling its ripples of pleasure riding up and down my spine.

"I'll uh . . . I'll check with Madame Matase when I ask about this." I held up the suit. "Thanks, Zee. I owe you one."

His grin wiped the confusion from his face. He glanced at the bed and back to me, the smile growing. "Or . . . you could pay me now?"

Yeah, no, I wasn't jumping into that bed with him again. Couldn't happen. Terrible idea. One time was enough—even if it wasn't, and never would be.

Truthfully, I'd have jumped his bones in a heartbeat, if I didn't have my own glamor to hold together. Last time, it had almost slipped its restraints. "I'll uh . . . I'll get this adjusted and come back . . . for the hair." I left the room, hoping this wasn't as weird for him as it felt for me.

After he'd woken from being starved, he'd told me to leave, and if I had left, we wouldn't have crossed the line. But I'd stayed, and now everything had changed between us—and maybe not for the better.

I should not have slept with him, but he'd needed it, and I hadn't been able to walk away from helping him.

It was done, and I had a tuxedo to try on.

A brief chat with Madame Matase revealed there was nothing wrong with the wards, and no reason why Zee ruffling my hair should trigger them. She took one look at me, made the adjustments to the tux with a flick of her hands—weaving fabric is a lot like weaving wards—and I retreated to my room to change.

The suit fit perfectly, and Zee was right about the hair—it was a bouncy, uncontrollable golden nest of somehow flat *and* curly fluff.

I found Zee in the bar, chatting with Tom Collins and one of the guests. His wings pricked as he saw me, and his hungry eyes drank me in. "Well, fuck me."

I smiled and nodded at the guest, then Tom, and fidgeted in the tux, restless under their scrutiny.

"No, Kitten, please do *fuck me*." He slid off the stool and closed the distance between us in a stride, then bowed his head. Did he mean to kiss me? Here, in front of everyone? But then his cheek brushed mine, and his words fluttered across my ear. "I can have you out of that suit and crying my name in ten seconds flat." He straightened, and patted my chest. "But as we're hands-off, I won't."

I'd almost choked on my tongue. "Uh, you said . . . about my hair . . ."

"Yes, I did. Come along then."

We said good night to the guest and headed up to his room, where Zee sat me on a stool in front of his multi-mirrored dressing table.

He propped his ass sideways on the dresser top, and gathered up an array of equipment and sprays, then set to work poking and stroking my hair. "So, what Adam Vex style are we going for? The professional, slicked-back, no-nonsense businessman, or the fun, friendly hotelier?"

"Just me, I guess."

"You said it's a business meeting? You need to look the part."

"Right." A kind of business.

"Who are you meeting?"

I swallowed and averted my eyes. "Oh, you know . . ."

Zee stilled. It took about three seconds for him to figure it out. "Oh fuck no."

And here it came. "It's just a dinner."

"You said it was *business*." He flung down the hairbrush. "A business meeting with Lord Fuck-Hard, without me? About what? The hotel? Why am I fucking surprised? He's clearly back then. Couldn't stay away. I wonder why."

"Zee, its nothing, really, I just . . ." He didn't know about the deal I'd made, and if I told him now—how Reynard could suck on a vein whenever he liked, just so long as he bought me dinner first—it would make everything worse.

His tail whipped back and forth, until he sat back on the dresser, trapping it. He folded his arms and harrumphed. "You just *what*, Adam?"

The last time he thought I'd cut him out, he'd gone back to Demontown, and to Sebastien, for reasons I still didn't fully understand. He was safer here, under the SOS Hotel roof. He'd come back from Demontown with marks on his neck and wrists. I wasn't supposed to talk about it, but that didn't erase the fact it had happened.

But I did need to be honest with him. "Look, when you were sick, I made a deal with Reynard. He would help me, and in exchange he got to . . . drink my blood when he liked, just so long as he bought me dinner first. Not a date. A business deal. That's what this is. Just business."

His eyes widened as I explained, and I couldn't tell if he was about to explode, or break down. He took a few moments to gather his thoughts. His eyebrows pinched together, and he said coolly, "No more deals without me. We're in this together. That was *our* deal when we started this."

"You're right." I shouldn't have cut him out. "I'll tell Reynard I can't go."

"No, go. You made a deal, and deals are sacred—it's fine." He snorted, took my hands, and drew me to my feet in front of him. "It would be a shame to waste all this. You look fucking amazing. Like a million dollars. Have fun. You deserve it. Just don't trust him, and don't let him make any more deals, or sweet-talk you with those fancy words of his, or accept any gifts. And don't let him fuck you."

"Uh, I don't think he wants that."

Zee's right eyebrow shot up. "Kitten, who is the lust demon?" He pointed at his own chest, then took my hand again. "Vampire Daddy wants to fuck you hard against a wall, trust me. He's all conflicted, for vampire-drama reasons. Once he gets over it, he's gonna hump you like a bitch in heat."

The imagery was . . . all wrong. But now it had taken root in my head. I definitely didn't want that. "I don't want that." Did I? "That's not . . ." I took my hands back and straightened my posh jacket. "That's not going to happen."

"Right." He booped my nose. "Go, have fun. I'll find a guest to fuck—I'm joking! Don't frown. The guests are off limits, blah blah. I promise to be good. Cross my heart and hope to die, stick a dick in my eye."

"That's not how that rhyme—never mind. You sure?"

"Yes, go. Run along." He air-walked his fingers. "I'm fine. I'll go fuck the pole, where I'm allowed to misbehave." He sat at the dresser and leaned back, raking his gaze over me once more. Undressing me with his eyes. I almost didn't go. Almost pounced on him, sprawled there, his body broadcasting all his finer points, ready to be devoured. He knew it too.

He might as well have been holding a sign that listed all the delicious, depraved things he'd do to me.

But if I stayed, and we . . . got personal again, it would make everything complicated. Not least because he wasn't starving. So he didn't *need* it, he *wanted* it, like I wanted him. But I wanted him differently to how he wanted me. Argh! Why was this all so darn messy?

"Just tell him"—he smiled, about to impart some demon wisdom—"if he hurts you, I will rip out his eyes, and shove them so far up his ass he'll be able to watch while I tear out his heart."

I chuckled, but he wasn't laughing. Just smiling in that precise way he did sometimes, with the points of his sharp teeth barely hidden. He'd meant every word.

"That won't be necessary." I was beginning to get the

distinct impression, that if Zee and Reynard met outside the hotel wards, only one of them would walk away.

"Adam." He called as I left the room. I turned back to see him still lounged on the stool, sprawled against the dresser and seemingly relaxed—but his tail wrung itself. "Be careful?"

"It's just dinner. What can go wrong?"

His smile twitched. But in the moments just before the door swung shut, that smile vanished, leaving his face cold.

Reynard had already proven himself to be helpful, and I owed him for saving Zee. He'd had plenty of opportunities to hurt us, but he'd saved us instead. This was just a dinner.

Besides, I was more than capable of looking after myself.

As it turned out, I was wrong.

About everything.

CHAPTER 2

"I JUST WANT to make things clear, so we're both on the same page and there aren't any misunderstandings. This dinner is part of our mutual arrangement, correct?"

"Yes, Adam," Reynard said, his voice smooth and deep, like warm honey drizzled from a hot spoon.

Well, that was a relief. "Good. Not that I . . . Not that we . . . I mean, it's not . . ." He blinked, and I sat a little straighter in my chair. This was just the deal. No other meaning, whatsoever. We'd eat, and then he'd suck on a vein. And that would be that. Simple.

"Good," I said again. Zee's words came back to me, about Reynard wanting to *hump me like a bitch in heat,* but he had to be wrong, because Reynard had never once alluded to any kind of sexual attraction. I, on the other hand, definitely *did* respond like a *bitch in heat,* whenever Reynard's fangs slid into my flesh.

A shiver trickled through me. The good kind. Nope. Could not think about that.

I'd initially thought the attraction was some kind of power, but I also knew, deep down, it was all me. I had a *thing* for Vampire Daddy, as Zee called him. But as it wasn't reciprocated, everything was fine, totally normal, and one hundred percent uncomplicated.

The restaurant around us sparkled with glinting chandeliers, shiny decor, and even shinier people. Most everyone here, probably knew who and *what* Reynard was, since he'd never attempted to hide his nature. Apparently, money could open doors that remained closed to the rest of the Lost Ones.

"Have you heard from Gideon Cain?" Reynard asked, while the server poured our wine.

"No, but it's only been a week." Gideon was probably sitting at the top of his tower, thinking up many creative ways of ruining me.

Reynard picked up his glass, tasted the wine, and thanked the loitering server, sending him on his way. "I fear Mr. Cain will not let this go."

I *knew* Cain wouldn't. He'd been very clear about not stopping until he got his hands on the hotel. Plus, there was the fact he suspected I wasn't human. Gideon Cain was a threat to everything I was trying to do with the SOS Hotel. He *did* need to be dealt with, but casual murder was largely frowned upon, and since I didn't want to ruffle any more feathers than we already had, I had no idea how to handle him.

"To that end, and considering Gideon's threat," Reynard continued. "I'd like to extend our arrangement."

What was he suggesting, exactly? "The arrangement regarding saving Zee?"

"Ah, no. I meant, I would like to stay at the hotel *indefinitely*." His silvery eyes sparkled, like everything else sharp and severe in the restaurant, but a hint of satisfaction tugged at one corner of his mouth. Or maybe I'd imagined it, since after he took a sip of wine, the smallest of smirks was gone, leaving his face in its default expression of mildly intrigued.

"Well, that's nice." I stroked my folded napkin, giving my

hands something to do while my thoughts whirled. Zee would not like it if Reynard became a permanent resident, and our business relationship was already under a lot of pressure. Having Reynard potentially lurking around every corner was additional tension the hotel didn't need. "But . . ."

He sighed and leaned back in his chair, fingers tapping the table. "Is it the demon?"

"The demon has a name. But it's not just Zee." Although, the fact he refused to say his name was part of the problem. "You've already done so much, and I certainly owe you, hence our arrangement, but any more than that becomes a bit *too* much. Don't you think? I mean, it's only been a little over a week. I wouldn't want you to make any hasty decisions. Perhaps when the amusement has worn off?"

Reynard gazed back, and I got the impression he wasn't often turned down. That cool gaze lowered the temperature in the room by a few degrees, until he smiled. "I'll concede defeat and be gone by the end of the month."

"I think that's for the best."

Our food arrived and we ate, while casually chatting about how Zee and I had renovated the hotel. Reynard seemed content to listen as I rambled, but by the third or fourth course of pretty food on square plates, he hadn't offered up any information about his life. The articles I'd found on him didn't mention family, kids, or anything outside of his business—just that he was a baron, but preferred to use the simpler title of Lord.

"So . . ." This was as good a time as any to try and pry some information out of him. "In the four years since the veil sealed, you've managed to build one of the world's largest tech companies."

His eyebrows lifted, and his expression stayed pensive, waiting for my question. "Are you impressed, Adam?"

Mercy, that low, dulcet voice. How did he do it? How did he make four words sound like, "*Suck my cock, Adam*?"

"I . . ." I shifted in the seat. "Well, most of the Lost Ones have struggled to find their place in this world, and there you are, a billionaire in just a few years. Yes, I'm impressed, I suppose."

Reynard stroked the stem of his wine glass, his gaze tracking the movement. What would it feel like to have those fingers skim me like that? So delicate, but also firm? "And how do you think I did it?" he asked.

"Oh, well, I haven't really—"

He leaned forward, and folded his arms on the table, closing the conversation down around us. The intensity of his gaze was like being pinned under a microscope. "Come now. You're no fool." His tone turned demanding. "Tell me how I built an empire in four years."

I had my suspicions, since I'd seen him in action outside the hotel, but didn't want to overstep by accusing him of something he might find unsavory. "Oh, well I . . ."

He chuckled and sat back. "It wouldn't be anything to do with my ability to persuade weak-minded people to do my bidding?"

"I had wondered if that might have played a part."

"Vampires are intolerable cheats. I didn't build a tech company, Adam. I took a promising start-up from a gullible, weak-willed human, and made it and his team mine. Your barman, Tom Collins, probably knows more about human technology than I do. I saw an opportunity, and stole it. Are you impressed now?"

What was I supposed to say? He smiled, as though all of this was just a friendly chat, but there was still an iciness to him that felt a lot like prickly anger. Zee would have known, since he could sense emotions better than I could. But even I sensed Reynard wasn't happy about his confession. He'd flung it at me as though wanting me to berate him.

The dessert arrived, just in time to break the tension, and I was beginning to wish we could leave already, since this whole charade was just foreplay for the main event.

I stabbed my fork into the little chocolate bomb and moaned at the delicious taste of its gooey goodness.

Reynard's unblinking stare latched onto my mouth. I swallowed.

At some point during the last few minutes, he'd gone from confrontational, to hungry-eyed predator, and I'd have lied if I told you the switch hadn't fluttered my heart in a weirdly good way.

He was doing that thing he did so well, where it seemed as though nobody else existed in his orbit, just me. Any moment now, he was going to steer me from this restaurant and make good on his promise to sink his fangs into my skin, and if it was anything like before, I'd be feeling his bite all the way down to my balls.

I was starting to feel it there now. I picked up my wine.

"Shit," he said. Which might have been the first time I'd heard him curse. His gaze had shot over my shoulder and landed on someone behind me.

"Victor!" a loud female voice declared. A beautiful woman approached Reynard's side, and bowed to plant a chaste kiss on his cheek. He stiffened, his expression shutting down and eyes going dull.

Dressed in a slim-fitting pencil dress, her fluffy white coat swamped her. But there was nothing small about her dagger-like smile, now aimed at me. "And who do we have here?" She straightened, and laid her hand on Reynard's shoulder.

"Rosanna, my dear, this is Adam," Reynard said, his voice tight. "Adam, do meet Rosanna."

"Hello." I rippled my fingers in a wave and picked up my

glass.

"My wife," Reynard said.

Oh fudge. I spluttered wine, sloshing it over the sides of the glass, onto the table and my lap. Moments ago, I'd been thinking about how good it was going to feel having Reynard's fangs in me. Imagined his fingers stroking up my . . . and now his *wife* was here?!

"Oh darling! There now." Rosanna grabbed a napkin and began to pat my chest down, then my lap, dangerously close to my manly parts. Her perfume swirled, filling my nose and throat. "Hm, aren't you tasty?" Her teeth snapped together an inch from my face. *Sharp* teeth. Fanged teeth.

"What?" I squeaked.

She laughed and flung the napkin onto the table, then wrapped an arm around Reynard's shoulders. "Oh Victor, you didn't tell me he was so adorable!"

He had a wife, and they'd talked about me? Although, from Reynard's dead-eyed glare, he didn't seem all that pleased by her arrival.

"You have a wife?!" I chirped, my voice stuck in a higher octave.

"Viccy, dear, I've been trying to reach you. Why aren't you answering my calls?"

"The hotel has poor reception." He smiled as she traced his jaw with a long fingernail.

Wow, this was . . . awkward. Why hadn't he mentioned he was married? It seemed important, although, as this dinner was just an arrangement, maybe it hadn't mattered. It wasn't as though we were dating. He didn't have to tell me anything about his life. I was just his food.

"It's almost as though you've been avoiding me," Rosanna went on.

"As though I'd dare." Reynard smiled.

"Oh well"—she beamed—"I see you're busy." Her silvery

eyes blinked at me, and there was that touch of hunger, as though her gaze alone could pin me down and devour me. Wait, was she trying to use some kind of vampire talent on me? Well, that was just plain rude.

"Rosanna," Reynard snapped. "Do not overstep your place, dear."

She turned her cool glare on Reynard. "I'll see you later. It was nice to finally meet you, Adam." She scooped my hand up from the table, and planted a kiss on the back of my fingers. "My, don't you taste delicious?"

I plucked my hand free. "It was nice to meet you."

She tittered a laugh and strode away, fluffy coat swishing.

We'd caused a stir, and half the other guests quickly pretended they hadn't all been watching the interaction.

Reynard's glare tracked his wife all the way across the restaurant, then fell to his wine glass. The restaurant noise bubbled up around us again, conversations starting over. But not ours. He didn't look up, didn't meet my gaze, despite my glare demanding it.

"Your *wife* seems nice."

He laughed, then raised his hand and caught the server's eye. "Check please, and hurry."

Dinner was over, then.

"We need to leave." He stood, and another server appeared with our coats. "Now."

Reynard flashed his black card, then had me out the door and bundled into a car so fast there wasn't time to ask why we were fleeing as though the restaurant was on fire.

"Duncan," Reynard said, addressing the driver. "My spouse made an appearance. You know what to do."

"Yes, sir," Duncan replied, and lurched the car from the curb in a squeal of tire smoke.

Okay, what was happening here?

Reynard glanced behind us, through the tinted back

window, then caught me watching him. "My apologies, Adam. I had no wish for you to see that."

"Your wife?"

He barked a laugh again. "Yes. Precisely." He dropped into the seat, huffed a sigh, and muttered mostly to himself, "We'll be safe at the hotel."

Safe? We were in danger? I glanced behind us, but saw only the glowing headlights from nighttime traffic. "What's going on?"

"Nothing. It's nothing." He cleared his throat and tugged on his cuffs. "Just a little . . . family issue."

I'd never seen him flustered, not even when we were attacked by Shadow. His wife's sudden and unexpected appearance had rattled him.

"I didn't know you had a wife."

"Did you need to?" He glanced over.

"No, I guess not." As I'd said to Zee, my lusting after Reynard was a me issue, not a Reynard problem, despite Zee's observations. The appearance of his wife had made some things clearer in that respect, but murkier in others—such as why he seemed concerned, perhaps even a little scared. He adjusted his collar, fingers fiddling at buttons, fluttering around with nerves.

"Lord Reynard," Duncan said, "We are being followed."

Reynard's top lip rippled in a very un-husbandly snarl. "If she reaches us before we arrive at the hotel, I cannot guarantee your safety," he told Duncan. Although he glanced at me too, so I figured the same applied. This, from a vampire who had fended off a shadowbeast and could go toe to toe with Zee. If he was afraid of his wife, then the rest of us should be too.

"Understood," Duncan replied, then dropped the car a gear and shot through a red light.

I gripped the seats, holding on, as Duncan swerved the car

around moving traffic as though it stood still. "Is she really so dangerous that we're—"

The car lurched sideways, and slammed into something harder than us—I didn't see what—and the world tipped, the insides of the car tumbling as though I'd been tossed in a drier. Air bags blasted. Metal screamed and groaned. But as quickly as it had begun, it was over, and we were back on all four wheels—windows smashed, air bags deflating. Duncan slumped behind the wheel, smooshed between floppy white bags, but groaning, so alive.

Reynard had gone.

He wasn't in the car.

I groped at the air bags, shoving them out of the way, and tried the door. But during the wreck, the frame must have buckled, crumpling the car like a can. The door wouldn't budge.

"Adam. You alright?" Duncan asked, twisting in the driver's seat.

The eye-watering odor of spilled gas wafted around us.

"Yeah, just . . . the door won't open."

Duncan smelled gas too, and fought with his belt to get free. I hadn't been wearing mine, and while I'd sustained some knocks, nothing was broken.

Where was Reynard? Had he been thrown free? I crawled across the back seat, tried his door, shoved it open, and tumbled out. The stench of fuel burned my nose and stung my eyes. I stumbled to my feet, and glanced around. Glass sparkled on the road. Several beaten-up cars littered the roadway, their passengers clambering free. Behind us, its front end buckled, a large fuel truck sat in a pool of shimmering liquid.

"My belt's stuck," Duncan growled.

The leaking fuel ran under our car. One spark would be enough to ignite it.

I grabbed Duncan's door but the frame had buckled

inward, cinching it closed. "Hold on." I reached in through the broken window and tugged at his belt, with no luck.

A whoosh sucked all the air around us, rushing it toward the tank truck. Dancing fire swooshed, gobbling up the pool in both directions, and raced toward us.

"What?" Duncan asked, seeing the fear on my face. "What is it?"

"Nothing." I tugged harder at the belt. It wasn't budging. Weren't these things meant to save lives?!

"Is that . . . Oh God." He'd seen the flames in the side mirror. "Get me out!"

I gave the belt an inhuman tug, snapping it in two, then grabbed Duncan under the arms and heaved him out. We bolted away, making it three strides. Fire roared in, blocking our exit, then snaking around behind us, locking us in. Heat sizzled my skin and burned my face. Flames danced in every direction.

Duncan coughed and covered his mouth with the crook of his arm. His wild eyes searched for a way out. There had to be one.

"There!" A small section had opened up. We dashed for it.

Baroness Reynard strode through the gap, the flames reflected in her mirror-like eyes. I figured her smile was not a helpful one.

"Run," Duncan urged. Which was all well and good, but run where, in a circle?

"Adam, Adam, Adam," she purred, heels clicking the asphalt. "You think I can't smell him on you?"

Him? Did she mean . . . Oh, this was about Reynard. "Oh, wait, I think you've got the wrong idea. Your husband and I, we're not involved—"

She moved so fast I didn't see her, and only knew she'd attacked when Duncan collapsed next to me, his neck bent at an odd angle. She'd killed him in less than a second.

"Darling," Baroness Reynard purred behind me. "He said you were *difficult*, said you were complicated, said it was *wrong*." She circled around and stopped in front of me. "Do you know what I see?" Her fangs flashed, shimmering with reflected fire. "Easy prey."

Fire danced around us, licking into the air, cutting off the outside world. Maybe there were people out there trying to dampen the flames? But if there were, they couldn't see us. Duncan was in all likelihood dead, and there was a high chance I'd be next.

It was just me—a human—and Reynard's vampire wife.

But I knew something she did not.

I smiled. "You should think carefully about your next move."

"Hm, his toys always taste better than mine." She strode up to me, and tipped my chin up, like she'd done with her husband in the restaurant. "I'm going to enjoy drinking you down." And now, there was no doubt she was using her talents to subdue me. "I can take you away, Adam. Isn't that what you want?" Her shining eyes lured me in, like they had her countless previous victims.

It would be painless. And perhaps a small part of me was so damn tired of hiding, that I wanted to let go of it all and fall into her arms. But I had more to fight for now. A dream to bring to life. A reason to live. I had friends. And people who relied on me.

Nothing and nobody would take what was mine again.

A dash of black signaled Reynard's arrival. He grabbed his wife by the neck, and slammed her down, doll-like, into the ground, cracking the asphalt. They shared a moment of marital understanding, pouring hatred into each other's eyes, and then she screamed and writhed like an angry cat.

"You don't touch him!" Reynard roared. "*Nobody* touches him. He's mine, as was made clear."

"Then fucking take him!"

Reynard growled, picked up his wife, dangling her several feet off the ground, and carried her toward the wall of flames. He thrust her into the fire. Her coat caught first—whoosh, up she went, blazing like a firework. Reynard held her in the fire, arm out, sleeve burning, but if he was in pain, his snarl made sure his face didn't show it.

Her wails began to choke off, but Reynard wasn't done.

He threw her limp, blazing body at the crippled fuel truck. The impact ignited the tank, blasting me back. Boiling flame spewed skyward.

I sprawled on the asphalt, knocked off my feet, and propped myself on my elbows. Flaming debris rained from the sky. The blast had extinguished the fire between me and the rest of the street, and there was Reynard, patting down his smoking arm.

He saw me, jogged over, and held out his good hand—as though his wife hadn't just threatened to kill me, and there wasn't some kind of vampire conspiracy to *take me,* and I was supposed to believe he was the good guy rescuing me?

"You know, I think I'll get an Uber." I scrambled to my feet without his help and set off walking.

"Adam?" He followed.

Sirens wailed nearby. There would be questions, and authorities, and problems I didn't need, all thanks to Reynard and his surprise marital woes.

"Adam, we had a deal."

"A deal?" I brushed grit from my torn, ruined tuxedo, all at once *sad*. This was Zee's tuxedo, and this evening was meant to be simple. Not another disaster. "I'll pass, since your wife just tried to kill me. Services rendered."

He had the nerve to appear annoyed. "That's not what we agreed."

"No, because I didn't know you had a wife. What else

don't I know?" I marched down the sidewalk. We weren't far from the hotel, just another block to go. We'd almost made it, before Duncan had wrecked the car. Duncan . . . who was now dead. I hadn't known him, but I did know he'd tried to get us to safety, and if Reynard had stayed in the car, he could have saved him from his wife.

I glanced over my shoulder. Reynard had gone. Good. I didn't feel much like getting up close and personal with someone who claimed I belonged to him, and clearly had some ulterior motive for getting close to me.

Zee had been right. Why hadn't I listened to him?

Because I'd wanted to ride Reynard's cock. It was true. I'd let my loneliness distract me.

I couldn't afford to make mistakes.

I stomped up the street, toward the hotel's glowing lights, and spotted a familiar silhouette standing on the porch. Reynard. Under the porch lights, I saw in more detail how his hair was all frazzled, and smoke wafted off his suit. His right arm was all pink and bacon-like. That had to hurt. My blood would probably fix him right up—except, he wasn't getting a drop.

Unless he said sorry.

"Are you going to apologize?" I asked, stopping at the foot of the steps.

"For saving your life?"

Saving my . . . *life?* He'd been the one to put me in danger! Plus, I could have handled his wife myself—although he didn't know that. I laughed him off and climbed the steps. "Never mind. Good night Reynard."

He snatched my wrist as I tried to pass him, jerking me to a stop. "I need our deal."

As I yanked my arm free, Zee appeared on the porch in a cloud of static, and *loomed*, which he did so well, using the height of his wings and horns to threaten for him. He exuded pissed-off vibes, even in his *Not Your Baby* crop top.

Reynard's glare flicked to Zee, his lips rippled in a snarl, but he backed up a step.

"Do you need anything, Adam?" Zee asked.

"No, I've handled it."

I pushed open the hotel door, and held it open for Zee. He lingered a little longer, tail lashing. The crackle of building energy tingled the fine hairs on the back of my neck and scattered goosebumps down my arms. The wards were readying for the inevitable smackdown.

"Zee?" I urged. The last thing I needed was another fight, and definitely not on the hotel steps. Zee turned his back on Reynard and followed me inside.

"You okay?" he asked, once we were inside the elevator.

I slumped against the back of the elevator car and tipped my head, blinking at the cracked light on the ceiling. "I ruined your tux."

"I never wore it anyway. Black and white ain't my vibe." He gave his wings a flick. "I'm getting notes of pissed off, a hint of sexual frustration, a pinch of disappointment, a sprinkling of regret, and some . . . guilt? All that, under a whole heap of burned fuel."

"Ugh. I should have listened to you."

"Wait, is Reynard bad news?" Zee exclaimed, acting shocked. "Did the vampire overstep your boundaries? Oh no, who could have seen that coming? Certainly not the sex demon with fabulous fucking fashion sense."

I smiled at his flouncing, my mood brightening.

He leaned a shoulder against the opposite side of the car. "Did he hurt you?" he asked, barely containing a growl.

"No, but his wife tried to."

"Someone fucking *married* him?! Are they insane?"

"I met her, and yes. Although, I think she's dead now. I'm

not sure."

"Sounds like a great night, then?"

"The best." I drawled, giving him a fake grin and two sad thumbs up.

"You know what cheers me up when I'm down?"

"Your drawer of jiggling dildos?"

"Actually, yes." He snorted. "But also getting fucked—actual fucking optional."

The doors opened and we exited together, heading for my room. And while the idea of drowning my feelings in a bottle did sound like an ideal way to finish the night, I had a feeling it might lead to more intimate encounters with Zee—and tomorrow, we'd regret it. "I'm going to shower the smoke out of my hair and go to bed. Tomorrow, everything will be better."

"Pfft. Boring, Kitten, but whatever. You sure you're good?"

I opened my door and flicked on the light. "I'm good."

The drapes over the window fluttered in the breeze, the window wide open. Strange, I hadn't opened it.

My tired-eyed gaze drifted to the dresser mirror . . .

ADAM VEX IS NOT WHAT HE SEEMS, had been scrawled on the glass, in what appeared to be lipstick. Or blood.

Oh dear.

Zee growled, and marched across the room. "That blood-sucker. He's dead. I'm going to fucking murder him to death the next time he steps outside the wards."

"I don't think this is Reynard." I poked at the writing. It was dry, and flaked off like blood. Leaving gifts in our rooms was Gideon's style.

When would the world stop hunting me?

I sighed, and eyed the room anew, feeling like a stranger in my own life. "Is that offer to get wasted still open?"

CHAPTER 3

AFTER I'D SHOWERED and changed clothes, Zee took me to his new favorite spot—a flat section of roof hidden among all the hotel's spires and pitches—and there, we lay on our backs, staring at the stars.

"We have fifteen guests," Zee said. "Fifteen people want to stay under our fucking roof. That's a good fucking thing, right?" He handed over the bottle.

"Yes." I took a swig of the tingling, slightly spicy wine . . . or spirit . . . or whatever potion Tom Collins had thrown together. Its contents were probably illegal.

"And I haven't fucked a single one. Aren't you proud?"

I snorted a laugh. "So proud."

"That's a record," he said, chuckling along. "When people come through the door at Razorsedge, there's one thing they want." He rolled onto his front and kicked his heeled boots in the air, wings gently rising and falling behind him. "They don't want that here. Well a few do, but . . ."

"Did you think they would?"

"Why wouldn't they? Have you seen me? Everyone wants

to fuck this. But here, I don't *have* to." He tilted his head, horn-ring glinting. "I have a choice."

I raised the bottle, saluting his newly discovered freedom, then handed it over again. He upended it, and glugged. We were probably on the wrong side of intoxicated, but it felt good, staring at the stars and not having to worry about something or someone crawling in my window to scrawl on my mirror.

"I can fuck the hurt away, if you'd like?" he said.

I frowned, without meaning to. His suggestion sounded . . . painful, and all kinds of wrong.

"Only if you want," he added, noting my expression. "Never mind. Whatever. Fuck off."

"You can do that?"

He shrugged, wings bouncing. "I usually charge a whole lot more, because, you know . . ." He circled a hand near his head. "It fucks me up. I was Razorsedge's most expensive fuckboy, with *extra* talents. Folks will pay a shit ton to fuck away their clinical depression and daddy issues. Beats fucking your shrink, right?"

I rolled onto my side and watched him stare at the bottle as though it had all the answers. He'd stopped swinging his legs, but his tail ticked against the roof. "Does it hurt? Taking someone else's pain."

He looked up and blinked big, emotive eyes. "Nobody has ever asked me that. Yeah . . . sometimes. Depends. If I let it."

"For the record, I won't ever make you do that." It seemed wrong, on so many levels, even if money changed hands— *especially* if money changed hands. How anyone could hurt him like that was beyond me.

Even if the hotel had only ever housed him and me, it would have been worth it, so he had a home that didn't exploit him. A safe place to return to. Somewhere he could be himself, and not worry about being hunted, or used and dumped on the sidewalk.

"You met Sebastien, huh?" he asked, his gaze flicking away, getting all twitchy. "When Shadow had me in the attic?"

"I did. He's uh . . . interesting."

"Yeah, he told me. I bet that went as well as a whore at a virgin's funeral?"

"Something like that." Sebastien had made it clear he thought he still had a hold over Zee, and that this hotel and I were just a temporary folly Zee would soon be bored with.

Zee laughed. "He's a fucking grade A asshole."

"Yeah, I kinda got that impression. You don't ever have to go back there, if you don't want to, you know."

He grunted an agreeable noise and handed the bottle back. "Yeah, except, there's this little thing called a contract —" He cut himself off, and his violet-eyed gaze danced every-where but at me.

"A contract?"

"Nothing." He waved me off and flopped onto his side, so now we were face to face. "I'm sloshed. Wanna fuck?" He smirked. "No strings. Just dicks in holes?" He mimed poking a finger through a hole, while his tail stroked up my leg, hitching my pant leg up from my ankle, trying to get inside.

I swallowed the last drops of Tom Collins's concoction and set the bottle aside, knocking it over.

His tail roamed higher, encouraged, since I'd crooked my knee giving it room to encircle my thigh. My heart thumped harder. Sex with Zee was a terrible idea. But I'd also had a really depressing evening, and was mostly drunk, and it wasn't as though we hadn't already gone there. So did it even matter if we messed around again?

"We can blame it on the booze," Zee said, shifting closer

still, his lips glistening under the starlight. "No harm, no foul."

Did I want to kiss those lips? Yes I did. Did I want to straddle his hips and have him fill me up? Yes, that too. The taste I'd had of him before had been necessary to help him heal, but this time, we both had a free choice, albeit an intoxicated one. He was my guilty pleasure, but did that mean I was using him?

His wings trembled. He pinched his lips between his teeth. His tail shifted higher, roaming between my thighs, and then rode over my hardening dick, rubbing through my clothes. The rest of him hadn't touched me, just his tail, as though we both knew he could whip it away and we'd laugh it off as folly. But I wasn't laughing, and neither was he. Need pulled at my skin, urging me on. But my heart wasn't immune like his. I couldn't indulge in sex without feeling, like he did to survive.

His tail cinched tight, clutching my cock, wrenching a gasp from my lips. Mercy. I should say no, but I wasn't going to.

"Fuck, you're beautiful under starlight," he whispered.

Oh, that was . . . kinda romantic. My soft heart did a little skippity skip while his tail rubbed my dick, its grip limited since I was still trapped in my pants. Desire thrummed in my body, hot and warm, reviving all my neglected needs.

Just a little taste . . .

His mouth nudged mine, teasing, promising more, and his tail rubbed harder, faster, getting me off, fraying my thoughts, so there was no hope of talking myself out of this, just the feel of him, the heat of him, the bone-melting *need* for him.

"Fuck, wait." He pulled back. "The wards don't reach out here." His tail, that had been getting busy with me, suddenly vanished. "I don't want to hurt you, but it's not that simple. I can't separate sex and feeding, if—"

I moaned, or whined, and scrunched his *Not Your Baby* top in my fists. "Shut up, Zee." He didn't know the wards not reaching us wasn't a problem, and thought he was seducing me since he wasn't able to switch off his allure.

I wet my lips, so close to telling him he had never, and *could never* enthrall me. But that would open a door to a conversation he wouldn't survive, so I dropped my hand to the impressive length of dick trapped behind his fly and gave it a rough, needy squeeze. Zee moaned, eyes rolling, wings shivering. I slammed a kiss onto his mouth, swallowing that moan, taking him into me like I was about to take his dick. He tasted like every forbidden thing—wicked sweetness and heated spice—and the kiss turned messy, rough, spiked with his sharp teeth.

"Gah, fuck, Adam, wait." His hand wedged between us, prying us apart.

Purple eyes searched mine, and there was doubt there, and maybe a little fear. I'd stop, if he wanted to. But then, whatever had him worried vanished behind his smile. "Fuck it."

His mouth slammed into mine, his hands poured around me, yanking me close, and all at once I was plastered against him, leg hooked over his, our cocks dry rubbing, still trapped in our clothes. His tail swooped up my back, pushing me against his hard chest.

Shifting my hips, I thrust my hand between us and tore at his belt, then plunged in and grasped his hot dick, rubbing it up my palm and wrist. Pre-cum slickened things up. He panted in my ear, against my cheek, my neck, wherever his kisses fluttered next. His hands and nails tore at my shirt, scrunching it up. Buttons popped, plinking on the roof around us. Zee's tongue flicked a nipple, then sucked. I arched, wanting more, but unable to think ahead to get it.

Then his tail dove inside my pants, slid under my balls, and probed my hole.

A riot of lust set me on fire, turning me into a burning pillar of need. I craved him, wanted to climb *inside* him.

Zee scooped me up, into his lap as he knelt. I hooked my legs around his hips, so now we were dick to dick, chest to chest, almost eye to eye, although he was taller, so had to peer down. His wings—spread behind him—crackled with purple lightning, sexual energy lighting them up in the dark. He thought I was beautiful, but I was nothing compared to him.

He snatched a little bottle of oil from his pocket, reached strong arms around me, and ripped the back of my pants in two.

"Hope these pants aren't important."

I didn't care about the clothes, just wanted them gone. His finger dipped, slicking oil between my ass cheeks. Then he cupped my ass, lifting me, so his dick, now free of his pants, slid under my balls, up my ass, and lodged at my hole. His wide tip pushed in. I moaned for more and tried to drive myself downward.

"Easy, Kitten," Zee purred, eyes blaze. "Don't want to hurt—"

"You can't hurt me," I growled, baring blunt human teeth in a snarl. "Do it. Fill me, Zee. I need it. I can take it. All of it."

His gaze danced across my face, reading me, as he fought with himself—to go slow, or do me hard. I knew what he wanted, and it wasn't soft and slow, or to whisper sweet nothings. It was animal. Primal. I needed his dick plunging into me, needed to come all over him, needed to make him *mine*.

His wings throbbed, ablaze now, burning up on the outside like I burned within.

"Fuck," he purred, his eyes widening. "What are—"

I slammed a hand over his mouth. "Never ask that. *Never*." I straightened, reached behind me, spread my ass and sank over his hard cock, making it very clear who was in control. As I took my hand from his mouth, his lips parted, dick sliding into me, widening, filling. His wings trembled, their tips stretched out. Tiny purple sparks rained from their edges.

Tilting my hips, I eased down, sheathing him inside—my cock erect between us—and began to rock. Tiny, tingling sparks danced, spilling like glitter across the remains of my clothes. Was that normal? Didn't matter, I was too lost to care.

Zee clutched my waist, holding me, urging me on, letting me set the pace. He dropped his head back, lips parted, lashes fluttered, and he *gorged* on us. With every roll of my hips, his wings pulsed and sparks rained. Somewhere, tangled up in the riot of lust, a small niggling sense of unease began to creep in. But Zee's breathing quickened. He was close to coming. I wanted that, wanted to take him.

I clutched his shoulders, adjusted my hips and worked him over harder, taking him deeper, feeling his dick probe parts of me that went beyond the physical. My straining cock stroked over his abs, leaking cum. It was glorious, messy, visceral.

My glamor writhed, trying to slip free from its restraints. I mentally clung to it, my rhythm stuttering, distracted. But it didn't matter. Zee moaned, long and low, and all at once, his spritzing glow throbbed around us both, consuming us inside it. He came with a shout, his face locked in bliss. I tipped forward, captured his mouth with mine, and rubbed my dick over his rippled abs. In three stokes, I was lost, and tore free of the kiss to cry out, my orgasm riding me. My thoughts rewired, and my skin burned, seeking to slip free and expose the very real, and very not-human insides of me.

"Fuuuuccckkk." Zee's hand clutched at my face. "Adam?"

I blinked, trying to focus on his blurred face. Uh oh.

"Adam? Shit, are you alright?" Why was he so dreamy and so far away?

"I uh . . ." Why were we floating in the dark? "I just . . ."

CHAPTER 4

I WOKE ALONE in Zee's bed, ragged and brittle, as though my skin was made of needle tips, and for a terrifying few seconds, I had no idea who or where I was. But I was still human, still had all my limbs in the correct places, and soft squishy human skin.

"Mercy."

My head throbbed, and my insides flip-flopped. Here came the hangover. Yanking Zee's sheets over my head, I buried myself among his pillows and drifted between sleep and wakefulness, my body pleasantly thrumming from the memory of his firm hands, and of me riding him.

A slamming door in an adjacent room jolted me awake for real.

I couldn't hide in Zee's bed all day.

A shower cleared my head, and after dressing, I ventured downstairs to the kitchen and grabbed a bowl of cereal from Chef Étrange. The shapeshifter took one look at my face and didn't ask how my night had gone—which was wise.

I ate my cornflakes, alone in the corner of the kitchen, hiding among the clatter of pans and a yelling chef. I was going to have to face Zee, sooner rather than later, and apologize—maybe? We shouldn't have . . . It was the booze. Just like Zee had said. Just the booze. Tom Collins had probably spiked it with something. He really needed to dial back on the drugs.

Taking a glass of water with me, I left the kitchen and headed into the lobby, then stopped and blinked at an explosion of red roses . . . *everywhere*. On the side tables, the front desk, stacked against the far wall. And more were being wheeled in. Zee stood at the front door, tail sweeping the floor, arguing with the delivery company to return the roses. He looked good, in his heels and tailcoat ensemble, with frilly cuffs and shirt collar—like a demon Mr. Darcy. Clearly, he was going for a historical vibe today.

I caught Madame Matase's eye and headed over to her. "What's with the roses?"

She pinched her lips together, and handed me a little card that simply read: *Sorry*. As I was still partially hungover, it took longer than it should for me to realize the flowers were meant for me. Reynard had sent them.

Zee strutted over. "I've trashed three crates already, and more keep coming. It's fucking obscene!"

It *was* a lot of flowers.

"Think of the poor, homeless human spawn who would love nothing more than to have all these flowers." Zee rolled his eyes. "Vampires are *so* selfish."

"I don't think homeless kids want roses, though. Wouldn't they prefer food and shelter?"

"If I were a homeless manbaby, I'd want flowers. *Good morning*, Adam." He leaned a hip against the front desk and trawled his eyes all over me. "How are you feeling, Kitten? Wild night, huh?"

"Uh, yes, about that—"

"It must have been off the fucking charts, because I don't remember a fucking thing. Do you?"

I swallowed. He was giving me an out, if I wanted to take it. We should discuss what had happened, because I wasn't entirely sure it had been *normal*. But now was not the time. Madame Matase had picked up the phone, but there were others milling about, *oohing* and *ahhing* at the mountain of roses. "No, nothing. Crazy night."

"Great." His teeth snapped together behind a smile. "Now, let's burn this bullshit attempt at groveling, and tell Reynard to fuck off out of our lives so we can get on with the business of doing business."

I did need to speak with Reynard, and make it clear our business arrangement was over. He'd outstayed his welcome. Even though we could really use his dollars in our bank account.

The woman who walked through the door at that moment, shouldn't have been walking at all after being spit-roasted last night. But there she was—Baroness Reynard—striding toward me, sunglasses shading her eyes, and new coat swishing around her ankles.

She stopped in front of us and pulled her sunglasses down her nose. "Ugh, a demon."

"Ugh, a bitch," Zee replied.

She huffed, and poked her sunglasses over her eyes again. "Adam, dear, may we talk?"

"Who's this now?" Zee asked me.

"Baroness Reynard," I drawled.

"The wife?!" Zee's grin turned predatory.

"Demon, avert your foul eyes, or I will peel them from their sockets."

Zee straightened, and stepped into her personal space. "Ooh, bitch, please. You feel that? That's our wards firing up.

But know this, fang fucker. The second you step off the front porch, you're fair game, and since you ruined my tuxedo—with my dear friend in it—you and me got serious beef. So much beef we'll be having a barbeque, and you're the main course."

She sighed. "Call off your pet, if you want to know the real reason Victor Reynard is slumming it under this roof."

Zee snorted. "Reynard is leaving. And we don't care."

"It's alright, I've got this, Zee," I told him. While we *were* about to throw Reynard out, it would be useful to know her side of the story, since Reynard had told me exactly nothing about himself, or his motives. She wasn't here to hurt us, or the wards would have given her a nasty headache as soon as she'd stepped through the door. As it happened, *I* was the only one with the crippling, self-inflicted headache.

"Let's talk in the bar. Zee, can you deal with the flowers?"

"You mean, burn Reynard's embarrassing attempt to smooth over his fuck-up? Of course, Adam. I'd be fucking delighted to."

Rosanna's eyebrow arched at Zee's easy dig, and she followed me into the bar, where only a few other guests chatted at a table. The bar was generally pretty quiet until later in the day. I sat at the bar, and Tom Collins breezed over, looking debonaire in a burgundy jacket and pinstripe vest over a white shirt.

"Bloody Bitch?" Tom said.

Rosanna removed her sunglasses and set them down on the bar. "Excuse me?"

"The drink?" Tom smiled, pretending he was innocent.

"Oh yes, thank you."

"Anything for you, Adam?"

I showed him my glass of water. "You and I need to chat about what you put in that drink last night."

"I'm sure I have no idea what you're referring to, and it definitely was not speed."

"Right."

We sat in uneasy silence as Tom fixed her drink, then scooted off to tend to his racks of multi-colored bottles.

"Why are you here?" I asked her.

"I thought you might appreciate some information about my husband, and what he's doing in this *delightful* hotel."

"You tried to kill me last night. Why should I listen to you?"

"Oh that was just"—she laughed—"a bit of fun. I forget how humans react badly to little threats of murder."

"A man died."

"They do that. Drop like flies, really. More than one died actually, since my beloved husband set me on fire, leaving me rather ravenous. I haven't needed to bathe in the blood of my victims since the sixteen hundreds. A blood bath does wonders for the skin. You should try it. You're looking a little peaky this morning." She sipped her drink, then set it back down to give me her undivided attention. "Now Adam, I'm going to give you the benefit of the doubt, and assume you're not as gullible as you look. Why would my husband, a man of the arts, a man of finer indulgencies and of impeccable taste, stay . . . *here*?" She gestured around, encompassing the peeling wallpaper, cracked ceiling, mismatched and frayed chairs, and the water-stained tables. The only shiny, new things, were the jukebox and the dancing pole—which said a lot about what our priorities were.

"It's a work in progress. And we don't ask our guests why they're here."

"Perhaps you should?"

I sighed, really not in the mood to be caught between two bickering vampires. "I'm going to be straight with you. I'm tired, and hungover, and I really don't like you much. So just get to the point."

"Very well. You're a gift, dear."

"A what?"

"A gift. For our queen. He's supposed to entrap you, bundle you up, and present you to her, and in exchange we earn our queen's favor. But my dear husband appears to be incapable of fulfilling his promises, which is no surprise as he's incapable of most things these days, including getting it up."

A thudding in my ears had grown louder and louder after the *gift* part. "Wait. Stop. He promised to gift me to his queen?"

"*The* queen."

"The vampire queen? Isn't she on the other side of the veil?"

Rosanna pinched her lips together. "Well, I wouldn't know anything about that."

I laughed. It was absurd. *She* was absurd. "Why me?"

"Initially, you were just an interesting human, since you'd opened this hotel for Lost Ones. But some information has since come to light, that might suggest you're a whole lot more than interesting."

My heart stopped, then kicked into motion again. "What information?"

"You've made some powerful enemies, Adam. I'd be careful who you keep close."

"What information?" I asked again.

She smiled and picked up her sunglasses. "Perhaps you should ask Gideon Cain?"

I smiled. "You should go. And take your husband with you. We're done here."

"Oh, we'll get him. Viccy has a date with the executioner." She eased off the stool. "I'll soon be Widow Reynard. Doesn't that have the perfect ring to it? Finally, I'll be free of my immortal enemy. Till death do us part."

"Wait, he's going to be killed?"

She shrugged, and popped her sunglasses back on. "Dear Adam. Did I not mention that's his reason for staying here? It's certainly not for the . . . *ambiance*." She screwed up her nose as she headed for the door. "If you see him, tell him it's time to come home and bow to the axe that will take his stubborn head."

I stayed sitting on the stool after she'd gone. Thinking. Going over what her words meant. Tom Collins eventually made his way over. "You know your problem, Adam?" he asked, stuffing a cloth into a glass and rubbing it dry.

I sighed. "Do tell me."

"You have a good heart."

And that good heart fluttered now. "You're more right than you know."

"The vampires want you dead. Or Reynard gets the axe. It's your life for Reynard's."

"Yes." I groaned and slumped on the bar. "I am aware . . ."

"Whiskey?"

"Probably not. I think I have a drinking problem."

"It's only a problem if you make it one," Tom said, nodding along. "But on the list of Adam Vex's problems, I'd suggest alcohol is way down. Barely a problem at all."

"You could say that." Not like the problem of Reynard. If I kicked him out, his vampire family were going to kill him. But he'd promised them *me* . . . as a *gift*. As though I were his to trade. As though I were an object. "That asshole."

Zee clanged through the doors, and joined me at the bar. "Baroness Bitch-Face has gone."

"Zee, we have a problem."

"Fabulous. Of course we do."

"It's Reynard."

He rolled his lips together. "Don't say it."

"He has to stay."

"Fuck. My. Life." He squeezed his eyes almost closed—to narrow, razor thin slits.

"Just for a little while longer, until I figure something out."

"Figure what out, Adam? Figure out he's not here for you, he's here for him?"

"It's not personal—"

"Isn't it?"

I held his gaze. "No." It wasn't. This was about my promise to protect everyone who stayed with us. Every name in the guest book was guaranteed a safe stay. Those were the rules. The deal we made with everyone who walked through our doors.

He breathed in, filling his lungs and expanding his wings, then sighed out. "Last night, you said you wished you'd listened to me? So listen now. Victor Reynard will *hurt* you, which means I will hurt him, and there's only one of us walking away from that fight. We have a good thing here, but it's only just begun. Don't crush the dream before it's had a chance to spread its wings."

He was right.

But also . . . wrong. "I have to speak with him. Join me?"

"Uh, don't make me talk to Victor Fuck-Hard."

"You don't have to talk, just listen. But it's important you're there. I need you there, Zee." I faced him, looked him in the eyes, and knew he wouldn't say no. "*Please*?"

His gaze flicked away, then he rolled his eyes, and his entire body, horns, and wings rippled in that same wave of resignation. "Why can't I say no to you? Every time. *Buy this hotel with me, Zee. Pretend you're not amazing, Zee. Lick my feet, Zee—*"

"I never said that."

He threw his hands up. "Fucking fine. But you owe me. And don't doubt how I will collect payment, Kitten."

I swallowed, letting a little grin slip through. "Promise?"

His pupils swelled and he leaned in, as though to kiss me. At the last moment, his cheek brushed mine, and he whispered. "I'm a whore for you, Adam Vex. And you totally asked me to lick your feet."

"I really didn't."

"Maybe I dreamed it?" He tilted his head, thinking. "Whatever. It was hot. You should ask."

I suspected he did remember last night, then. Because it had suddenly become all I could think about—how I'd rocked in his lap, how we'd lit up the sky.

Breathing in and clearing my throat, I snatched up my non-alcoholic glass of water. "Let's go see if Reynard is in."

After a tense elevator ride, we knocked on Reynard's door. He probably wasn't in. He'd had a rough night too, and then there was the tech empire to preside over. "Doesn't sound like he's in."

Zee narrowed his eyes and leaned a little closer to the door.

"You could *poof* inside?" I suggested. Zee materialized in my room all the time.

He recoiled. "What if he's jerking off?!" Then he seemed to reconsider, eyebrows lifting, coming around to the idea.

"No, you're right." I shook my head. "It's a breach of privacy."

He glanced at me and knocked again, rapping his knuckles against the wood. "*Feels* wrong inside. You got a spare key?"

"There's a master key in the safe. I can—"

He grabbed the handle and jolted it down, popping the door open. So much for privacy.

"Or, we can just break in." I followed Zee into the gloom. The drapes were closed and the lights off. Heavy, stuffy air and the smell of smoke, hung like a mist in the room. Thankfully, we hadn't barged in on Reynard sleeping—or doing *other* things—the bed was empty, sheets just a little wrinkled but not slept in.

"Okay, we should probably go," I suggested.

Zee made his way around the bed and bounced back. "Fucking Hell's balls."

I hurried around the bed, hoping it wasn't another dead body. Maybe Reynard had gotten hungry, snacked on some takeout, and left his victim in his room? I *had* turned him down, and he'd seemed pretty desperate, so . . .

But no, it wasn't a body. It was Reynard. Out cold, on his back, sprawled *like* a corpse. His arm was all burned and scabby still, and his jacket reduced to ashes.

"Oh deary."

CHAPTER 5

"IS HE BREATHING?" I asked.

"Hopefully not." Zee poked Reynard with his boot, getting no response.

"Zee!" I dropped, and jabbed at the pulse in Reynard's neck. "Do vampires have pulses?" I couldn't find one. "Zee?!"

"Meh." He folded his arms and leaned against the bed post. "We could pretend we didn't see him and leave?"

"I'm not leaving." He didn't seem dead, just limp, but still warm, and obviously unconscious. "Help me get him onto the bed." Zee didn't move. "He helped *you.* If he hadn't, you'd be dead."

"Fuck, fuck, fuck, fuck." A slew of *fucks* continued to fall from Zee's lips, as he scooped Reynard up and plonked him on the bed as carefully as throwing down a bag of trash. I glared. He rolled his eyes.

"What do we do?" Perching on the edge of the bed, I undid the first few buttons of his collar, not really knowing why, but maybe it helped. His arm was all bacon-like and badly burned. Otherwise, he seemed okay. No other wounds. He was pale, but he'd always been pale.

"Call his wife back here?" Zee suggested, loitering at the foot of the bed. "She can have him."

"No, she wants him dead."

"Huh. Maybe Mrs. Fuck-Hard ain't so bad."

"Zee," I snapped. "If Victor Reynard dies in our hotel, how will that look?"

Zee pouted. "Shit. Damn. Fuck."

"Very shit, and uh . . . the rest. So stop moaning and help me make him better."

He gave himself an all-over shake, and groaned. "It's blood. It's always blood with suckers. The virus eats their own red blood cells, so they have to steal them from everyone else. Whatever happened on your date last night knocked him out."

"His wife came at us. They fought. He set her—and his arm—on fire."

"Yeah, that'll do it." He picked at his nails, uninterested.

So, when Reynard had said he needed our deal, he'd really *needed* it, not just wanted it. And I'd shrugged him off. Granted, his wife had tried to kill me, but her appearance had been a surprise for him too. Even if he did have ulterior motives for staying with us. Which I sort of expected, but didn't want to acknowledge, with everything else happening.

Also, we'd needed his money.

Zee's gaze flicked up. "Open a vein, Kitten."

"What?"

"If you want a vampire to get on his knees and beg, open a fucking vein." He pulled a switchblade from his pocket and tossed it over. Why did he have a knife on him?

"Knife play," he said, answering my unasked question.

Of course it was. I flicked the blade part open.

"Cut across your wrist, not up. I ain't dragging your peachy ass to the ER."

I sighed out, and pressed the edge of the blade to my

wrist. The wards wouldn't kick in, as this was self-inflicted. Slowly, I drew the blade across my skin. Blood swelled in its wake, then dribbled onto Reynard's shirt.

Zee moved up to my side. "Hold your wrist over his mouth."

"Have you done this before?"

He side-eyed me. "I don't *do* suckers, remember?"

That wasn't technically an answer, but I did as he'd said, and held my forearm an inch above Reynard's mouth. Blood spilled over his cheek, then his lips.

"If he's not too far gone, he'll—"

Reynard lurched up from the pillow, buried his fangs in my wrist, then tore them out and moaned, writhing. Pain flash-burned up my arm. "Ow!"

Blood dribbled faster now, spilling onto his face, his chin, his lips. He licked it off, and lunged a second time, eyes wild. Then again, yanked himself back.

"It's the wards." Zee sprang into action and pinned Reynard down by the neck. "Every time he goes for you, they slap him down. Bleed *into* his mouth, Adam. Quickly. I might not be able to hold him."

This was a lot trickier than I'd thought. And weirder. I squeezed my bleeding wrist, but as Reynard thrashed against Zee's hold, the stream of blood ended up all over Zee's arm—and all over me and Reynard—but not in his mouth, where it needed to be. I climbed onto the bed and straddled Reynard's bucking thighs, pinning him down there too. I hovered my throbbing arm over his snarling lips, and bled.

Finally, enough got through for him to snap out of his murderous thrall and realize we weren't hurting him. His gaze skipped to Zee, who glared back—not helping with the harmless, safe vibes I was going for.

When Reynard's gaze found my face, his entire body softened under me—well, most of it. Not the one, very hard part, prodding my inner thigh.

A part I was definitely not thinking about with Zee *right there.*

Reynard's tongue lapped up the dribbling stream of blood, painting his lips and chin scarlet.

"Alright, you're done," Zee said, and nodded at me to stop.

I clambered off, grabbed a towel from the bathroom, and wrapped my wrist. By the time I'd returned, Zee was leaning over Reynard, speaking in a voice so low I didn't catch the words. An awkward, tension-filled silence settled over the room.

Zee straightened, letting Reynard up. Although he didn't move. He just lay there, breathing hard, staring at the ceiling, while I tried not to notice how his cock tented his tailored pants.

Zee spotted it too, and smirked. He poked his tongue into his cheek and mimed sucking a dick, which was definitely not appropriate.

"Maybe I should leave you two alone?" Zee purred.

"Don't!" I propped my ass against the dresser and cradled my hot wrist close.

He flopped into a chair beside me. "I'm not going anywhere. He's barely coherent. And you're bleeding. Even if I have got a hundred and one better things to be doing than babysitting a vampire—like arranging my killer wardrobe by vibrancy—I'm staying. But *you* can go. Fix your wrist up."

"Leave you alone with him?"

His gave his horns a shake and ruffled his hair between them. "What do you think I'm going to do? The wards won't let me have any fun, and there's no use in both of us twiddling our thumbs, waiting for him to stop thinking with his fangs."

He had a point. "You sure?"

"Or we could cuff him?" He grinned. "I bet he's into it. He's a total top daddy, into chains and whips."

"We can't cuff guests to their beds, Zee. Even those you don't like. No cuffs."

He pouted, and slumped deeper into the chair, wings and tail flopping over the sides. "You're exactly this much fun." He showed me a zero with his finger and thumb—then poked a finger through it and grinned.

Oh my stars, save me from horny demons and hungry vampires.

"Alright, I'm going, but don't . . . molest him."

He gasped. "I'm not touching Vampire Daddy. Cross my heart and hope to die, stick a—"

"Yeah, okay. I get it. Just come and get me when he's normal again."

It still felt strange leaving Zee in the same room with Reynard, especially as Reynard wasn't coherent. But I trusted Zee not to touch someone who wasn't awake enough to consent. He *knew* that was wrong, even without the wards preventing anything untoward from happening.

Madame Matase helped fix my wrist with butterfly strips, and since I was too wired to rest while Reynard recovered, I tended to the hotel for the rest of the day.

Tonight, with Reynard back to his normal self, we were going to sit down and talk it out. For better or worse.

Till death do us part.

It was him or me.

But there was a third option . . .

In the evening, as our time to meet up approached, I found Zee sitting alone in the bar, nose buried in a book, and upon closer inspection saw it was the *Wilson's Guide*. The jukebox bubbled out a jazzy swing tune that gave the bar a party atmosphere, and Tom Collins was spinning drinks and telling his customers to fluff off—so everything was normal there.

I pulled out a chair at Zee's table and sat. "What are you studying?"

"It's a crime, I'm not listed under the Z's. There should be a whole fucking page devoted to me. Instead, we get Zouyu —a vegetarian tiger shifter. Pfft, please."

"What would yours say?" I asked, playing along.

"Zodiac. The one, the only, the most beautiful example of an incubus the human world has ever seen. Known for impeccable fashion sense"—he swept a hand at his red and black corset—"no gag reflex"—his eyebrows skipped—"and for being an absolute fucking master at edging."

I had no idea what edging meant, but he was clearly proud of his skill at it. "Any warnings?"

He tossed his head, throwing his gaze up, thinking, then counted on his fingers. "The weak may orgasm on sight of this devilish prince. Exhaustive stamina. High maintenance— because perfection ain't easy. Annnnd . . . ? Cock's too big?"

I barked a sudden laugh and we chuckled together, until Zee tossed the tattered book onto the table between us and remarked, "Did you know fae can't lie?"

"I did know that, yes." Which was why I'd trusted the one who'd sold me a *broken* AI bartender.

"Yet they're the biggest fucking con artists in the city. A friend of mine, Ramone, lost his right horn to a fae. The skinny wraith wanted to grind it up to make some kind of fucking face powder."

"Oh, uh, yuck."

"I know, right. People think demons are fucked up, but I don't rub bits of fae all over my face. Although, there was that one time . . ." He trailed off, then shook himself back into the room. "Anyway, the D's are missing."

"It's not like you not to find a *D*."

He leaned in, purring agreeably, and propped his chin on his fist. "You're feeling better, I see."

I was, in fact, feeling much better. The day had started off rough, but I'd begun to feel a lot like my normal self, despite the butterfly bandages running across my wrist. I'd wrapped them up, so my quick healing wasn't so noticeable.

Zee poked the book's cover. "But yeah, whole page of *D*s, torn out."

"It's an old guide. We inherited it when we bought the hotel."

He shrugged and sat back. "Half of it's PR bullshit anyway. Rumor is, the vampires spun some fuckery on Mr. Wilson and had him write it the way they wanted."

Speaking of vampires. "Is Reynard joining us, like I asked?"

"He said he was." Zee leaned back and kicked his boots up onto the table. "Whether he does or not after we both saw that fucking disaster, who knows."

"Yeah, it was difficult. I doubt he ever wanted either of us to see *that*."

"Pfft, it's nothing I ain't seen before. We get suckers at Razorsedge sometimes, even after Seb banned them. The hungry ones sneak in, trying to suck on the merch. They get desperate, like crack addicts."

"So you *have* dealt with it before?"

"Occasionally." He flicked a hand, as though it was nothing, taming a vampire. "One tried to get frisky with me. Took three of us to hold her. His lordship wasn't that far gone, or I wouldn't have been able to pin him down."

"At least we have the wards." Without them, there was no doubt Reynard would have torn into me.

"I'm getting a drink," Zee said. "Want one?"

I showed him the water bottle I'd brought along. "Still hydrating after . . . last night."

"You know, the best way to cure a hangover is more alcohol." He scooted from the table and chatted with Tom at the bar, then a guest who sidled up to him and wanted a selfie. Her phone didn't work, so he took a pen and signed a *Z* across her bulging chest instead.

"Adam." Reynard appeared at the table, making me jump. The music and general chatter had muffled his sneaky approach. "May I sit?"

I nodded, and gestured at the free chair. He seemed a little stiff, but otherwise more put together than the last time I'd seen him.

Zee returned with his drink and glared at Reynard. "Vampire."

"Demon."

"I hope this won't take long since there's a pole over there with my name on it." Zee dropped into his chair, and kicked his boots up onto the table again, his wings and his *everything* taking up the space of three men.

Reynard narrowed his eyes, and Zee grinned.

"Before we start," I said. "Both of you need to agree not to fling insults at each other or set off the wards."

"Agreed," Zee said, suspiciously easily.

"Acceptable." Reynard lifted his chin and sat upright, as though on trial.

Zee's tail twitched on the floor, in the corner of my vision. He was trying very hard to behave, and I appreciated it. Likewise, I supposed, Reynard didn't want to be sitting at the table with Zee either. We were already making progress.

"We had a visit from your wife, while you were indisposed," I told Reynard. His dark eyebrows shot up. I plowed on. "She said I was to be *a gift* for your queen. That you gifting me would inflate your status, and since you hadn't produced me—presumably, either dead or near to it—you'd be executed on your return home."

"*Fuck*," Zee breathed. He hadn't known all the details. "I take it back. You both need to fucking die, but that bitch especially."

"That's my wife—" Reynard snapped. Then smoothing down his shirt, he said, "But I agree. I've been trying to kill her for several hundred years. She's quite robust."

"True love." Zee grinned. "The shine wears off after a few years, huh? Then you want to stab each other's eyes out. The tricks tell me all about so-called love while I'm getting them off." He mimed pumping a cock.

A disgusted growl rumbled through Reynard. "It was never *love*, demon," he snarled. "We don't marry for something as frivolous as love. We marry for status, wealth, lands, and the queen's favor. I lost all of that when the veil sealed, trapping us here."

"Oh, boo-fucking-hoo. We all lost lives back home, cupcake. You think I've always fucked for cash?"

"I doubt you were always paid," Reynard quipped.

"Fuck you. I had a life, a family. I *was* someone." He swallowed, and instead of continuing, showed Reynard his middle finger.

"Yes, I'm sure you were the same juvenile, attention-seeking whore you are now."

"Like those things are problems? I know what I am." He grinned, and swept a hand through his hair. "You're a cock-whipped sucker with no power, so desperate to lick his queen's cunt he'll pluck some random human out of the spotlight and dump him at her feet. You're the most pathetic creature I've seen this side of the veil, and believe me, the worst of the worst crawl through Razorsedge's doors."

I was going to have to step in and stop this before—

"Adam's not random though, is he?" Reynard said.

Zee clamped his lips shut and sat back, arms crossed. His tail lashed.

Reynard glared.

Zee glared back.

What was happening here? Why and how had the discussion come around to me?

"Are you, Adam?" And now Reynard's gaze slid to me.

"What?" I chuckled. "I'm just me."

Reynard slumped back too, and picking up an SOS Hotel coaster, he played with it between his fingers.

Wow, this just got awkward.

I huffed through my nose. "Don't make this about me, *Victor*."

At the sound of his first name, he looked up. "I apologize. For all of it," he said. "For coming here with malicious intent. For putting you in danger. For not telling you sooner, when it became clear you would listen. The fact is, as soon as we met, I suspected I'd made a mistake in offering you as a gift, which left me in the rather difficult position of not being able to deliver on a promise. My wife is right, and so is the demon. I have nothing left to offer the queen, and I've broken my word. I will face the consequences."

"The consequence is the axe," I reminded him.

"Yes." He swallowed with an audible click. "It is our way."

"Good riddance. Fuck off." Zee rippled his fingers in a wave. "Bye."

Reynard glared through his lashes. "You are intolerable."

"And you got caught bullshitting to your queen. Ha. Ha. Sucks to be you. Oh wait, you *do* suck, in every way. Loser."

"Zee," I warned. "He's being honest."

"His wife nearly made good on his little gift idea, Adam, or had you forgotten that part, since you're buying what His Grand Lordship is selling?"

"I'm not . . . that's not . . . that's not what we're talking about here." I glowered at Zee. He hadn't needed to *go there.*

Zee winced, turning his face away. "Shall we just skip to the part where you let him stay because you're too fucking nice, and he'll take advantage of your bleeding heart because he's a blood-sucking psychopath—"

"Enough!" That came from me, surprising us all—and the people at the nearby tables.

Zee recoiled. "Fuck this." He stood, knocking his chair back. "And fuck you." He pointed at Reynard. "I don't have a heart as kind as his. Like I told Baroness Bitch-Face, I will absolutely fuck you up if you ruin what I have here with Adam. Money and gifts can't buy Adam. And you know as well as I do, Adam is worth more than you, *Fancy Daddy*, can afford. Don't make the mistake of thinking I'm only good for fucks. You have no idea the nine levels of shit I've crawled through to get here, and I will absolutely take you and your leech family out." He cocked a hip, punctuating his tirade, and blew Reynard a kiss.

Reynard, to his credit, sat and absorbed it all without retaliating.

Zee strutted off, heels stabbing the floor, then he poofed away, vanishing in a cloud of sparks.

I let his words settle around us. The jukebox played, and the people in the bar started up their conversations again, after Zee had briefly stolen the show. "He's not wrong," I said.

"Perhaps not. But will you allow me to stay?"

"I'm considering it. You're paid until the end of the month. That's a few days away. I'll have your answer by then."

He sighed, and turned his face away. "When I arrived, I did not expect to find . . . you. I am sorry."

"You didn't expect to find me in my own hotel?"

"More accurately, I expected to find a foolish, misguided human, who had opened a hotel for predators who would likely eat him within twenty-four hours. But that's not at all what you are."

Everyone had a theory, didn't they. Everyone wanted a piece of me. All the pieces on the game board danced in a circle, with me at their center. *"I'm not what I seem . . ."* I echoed Gideon's message on my mirror. Reynard was desperate. His own family wanted him dead. He'd run out of places to run to. I knew what that felt like.

I leaned forward, and he leaned in too, sensing a change in our ambiance. "If I were to help you with your wife problem, would you help with my sorcerer problem . . . *permanently*?"

He looked up, black lashes lifting, highlighting silver eyes. "Are you proposing a new deal?"

"Not a *new* deal." Zee had said I wasn't allowed to make any new deals without him. "Just adjusting the terms of our old one."

He extended his hand, and I wrapped my fingers around his. "I agree, Adam Vex."

I nodded, and we separated our hands. A scattering of glittery sparks rained on the table, then vanished. That was . . . new. And probably nothing. "So, how *do* we dispose of an ancient vampire baroness?"

"I was hoping you might have some ideas, as after several centuries, I've exhausted all mine."

I had a few. But it was dangerous. I'd need Zee's help. Although, I was fairly certain, no demon was going to pass up the opportunity to ruin a vampire's day. Or their life.

CHAPTER 6

ZEE WAS IN THE LOUNGE, surrounded by guests, spinning them an x-rated tale about a wild night he'd enjoyed with an eight-legged octo-shapeshifter and multiple holes. I caught his eye. He left the group, laughing, and sauntered over.

"Don't talk to me about Fuck-Hard. It'll ruin my mood."

"Oh. Okay . . . The weather is nice outside. Warm for this time of year, don't you think?"

Zee narrowed his eyes. "Kill me now. What is it? I assume you want to ask something, from the way you're all . . . twitchy."

"I'm twitchy?"

"Your eyes get fucking shifty when you're about to ask something you think you shouldn't. So, what is it, Kitten?" He leaned against the back of a couch and folded his arms, patiently waiting.

"Do you, uh . . . happen to know any demons who, erm . . . perhaps are morally solid, but also legally, erm . . . challenged?"

He blinked. Then laughed, loud enough to draw a few salacious glances our way.

His laughter faded, and his face got all muddled. "Oh shit, you're serious."

He looped an arm around my shoulders and guided me from the lounge, through the lobby, and into the conference room, perhaps sensing the conversation was sensitive. "Something you need to get your cute, fluffy blond head around, is that human laws are a bunch of words demons don't much care for. So, do I know demons who will break those laws? Kitten, that's every fucking demon this side of the veil. You're gonna have to narrow it down."

"I sort of"—I thrust my hands into my pockets—"adjusted my deal with Reynard. So *we* help dispatch his wife in exchange for *his* help dealing with Gideon Cain."

Zee's left eyebrow shot up. "What kind of help?"

I shrugged. Hands still in pockets. "People die all the time?"

His left eyebrow arched, and the gold loop in his horn jiggled. "And you want to ask if I know anyone who will help you murder a vampire? Well, fuck, just come right out and say it, baby." His grin grew, stretching over sharp teeth. "That's an average Friday night in Demontown."

"Oh good." I'd been worried he wouldn't be on board. From his voracious smirk, I needn't have.

"Violence is always the answer," he purred. "Unless it's sex."

"Erm, I'm not sure that's true—"

"Get your coat, I'm taking you out on the town."

I followed him out of the conference room. We were going to Demontown. Hopefully, it would go better than my last few visits. Although, with Zee at my side, what could possibly go wrong?

Music throbbed through Razorsedge's thick walls. There was no line outside, but there were a few scantily clad female demons advertising the club's services. One waved at Zee, then blew me a kiss. "Oh, what a cutie," she crooned, riding her hands up from her waist, over her breasts.

"Hands off, Velvet, he's with me," Zee told her, pushing through the club doors.

A chorus of voices erupted. *"Zee! Baby! You're back!"* All manner of colorful demons emerged from corners and corridors, tails and wings flicking. *"Missed you, bitch! Baby, you're fine! Come over here, slag."* Zee soaked it all up, as you'd expect, laughing and jibing with them, while I watched on, bedazzled by all the colorful outfits, a few more revealing than others. I wasn't sure what I'd expected, having only visited in the day when the club had been closed. But clearly —and obviously—Razorsedge came alive at night.

We ventured deeper into the club, pushing through crowded corridors, then emerged onto a dance floor with a raised stage, where a slim female demon wrapped herself around a pole in time with the music.

"So, we have the main stage here," Zee explained, draping himself against a bar. "The studio's out back, where we film. And then there's the warren."

"Warren?"

He cocked his head. "A hall with private rooms off it, for some one-on-one time."

Right. Well, it all seemed fairly . . . civilized, so far. I'd imagined something more like a crazy free-for-all, with rowdy demons all over. There *were* demons in the audience, but other Lost Ones too, and a few humans with . . . collars on. Oh . . . Wait . . . The humans were wrapped up in those skinny, leather belt–like outfits, like the one Zee had in his wardrobe. Ah, they were *demon bait*. Wow, okay. Since I'd been called demon bait more than once, I clearly looked as though I should be wearing a collar and paraded around with my ass out.

I mean . . . I wasn't entirely opposed to the idea.

"You're staring, Kitten."

"What? Yes. No. What. I . . ." I swallowed and turned my back on the show. There was no escaping it though, because the wall of mirrors behind all the glass bottles reflected *everything*.

"You want a drink while we wait for Ramone and Cherise to finish up?" Zee asked.

"Oh, sure."

"Good, because you're giving off a heady mix off lust and fear, which is tickling all the wrong senses, and if you don't fuckin' relax, babes, a few demons will be all over you like chum in a shark tank."

Oh right. I breathed in and out, and tried to calm my galloping heart. "Who are Ramone and Cherise?"

Zee waved over the barman. "Two friends who are going to help us fuck up vampires without asking why. They despise suckers."

He'd mentioned Ramone before, as the demon who had lost his horn to a fae.

"Zee, baby," the demon behind the bar drawled. Small, as demons went, he wasn't much larger than me, and wore a glittery sequined suit that had him sparkling under the club's party lighting. "Who's the demon bait?"

"Adam," Zee introduced me. "Be nice, this is his first time. Adam, say hello to Ben Dover."

I was sometimes naïve, but not *that* naive. Ben was clearly not his real name. "Hey."

"Fuck, you're fresh." His big brown eyes undressed me.

"Zee treating you right? Because if he ain't, you can come visit me anytime, peaches."

"Fuck off, Ben," Zee laughed. "Adam's off limits."

"Shame. He's got the whole power-bottom vibe goin'." Ben sucked on his teeth and eyed me like I was a popsicle he wanted to wrap his forked tongue around.

Zee chuckled. "Two *Bruisers*, Ben. Fucking spike our drinks an' I'll rip your wings off."

"What happened to Fun Zee?"

"Fun Zee is also High Zee, and High Zee is not here right now. I have a guest. I'm *behaving*."

Ben nodded, understanding, and set about fixing us those drinks. Un-spiked.

I had two ways I could handle this. Take offense at *everything* and bristle. Or go with the flow. Since this was Zee's world, his life, and I didn't want to offend him or anyone here, I chose going with it. I trusted him, and if these were his friends, then I trusted them too. Mostly. A bit. Not all that much.

"Zodiac, you whore!" someone slurred, and lurched out of the crowd. A big, furry guy, with a barrel chest and legs as thick as tree trunks stumbled toward us. "Get your tight ass on my lap, bee-atch."

Zodiac thrust a hand toward the man's face. "Not working tonight, Abe."

But Abe clearly wasn't thinking straight. Or maybe he was always a jerk. He batted Zee's hand aside and staggered against him, knocking Zee into me. "You too good for my cock, Zodiac? I'll pay double."

Zee's tail rattled a warning as he bared his teeth in a hollow grin. "Fuck. Off."

Zee could handle himself. But the night I'd found him, he'd been tossed out like trash, and it was people like Abe who had done that to him. He was calm, but my blood began to simmer.

"Easy, guys," Ben warned, placing our drinks on the bar.

There were no wards here, probably because the whole issue of consent got real murky in a sex club. Reynard and I had met the gargoyle security guard, but there didn't appear to be any security nearby at the moment.

Abe shoved a hand into his pocket, grabbed a bunch of dollar notes and shoved them at Zee's chest. "With the money I've paid you in the past, I should fuckin' own you by now. Get on your knees and suck me dry—" Abe's hand dropped, going for the goods between Zee's legs.

I tensed, desperate to jump in and shove Abe off.

Zee grabbed Abe by his thick neck and slammed him head first into the bar, smooshing his face into the glossy bartop. Our drinks rattled. Abe grunted. Zee leaned in, pinning Abe down as the big man groaned and twitched, semiconscious. "Don't touch the fucking goods without permission." He hauled Abe upright, and shoved him away from us. "Sober up."

Abe grumbled, rubbed his red face, spat a snarl, then stomped off.

"Lupine shifters." Zee sighed, wings drooping. "Just another fucking day in paradise." He picked up his drink and downed it in one.

I wrapped my fingers around my glass, but didn't feel much like drinking. When I'd found Zee, we'd been strangers. Then we'd fixed up the hotel together, side by side, and he'd brought life and laughter back into my life. I'd gotten to know the real Zee behind all the snark and strutting. More than that, I cared. He didn't deserve to be handled like a possession.

"Stop feeling sorry for me. I don't want your pity," Zee

said, holding out his empty glass for Ben to refill it. He'd sensed my mood souring.

"Sorry."

"Uh. Don't apologize either. You're ruining the vibe."

"I can't help it if I get . . . I just can't help it."

He huffed through his nose, and *now* his tail lashed.

"Shit's gotten a bit tense lately," Ben told Zee. "Seb was an asshole after the last time you left."

"When isn't he?"

"More of an asshole than usual."

Zee lifted his gaze, licked his lips, met Ben's stare, and huffed as a glimmer of mutual knowing passed between them. Sebastien had clearly made the others pay for Zee's leaving.

Maybe it hadn't been a good idea to come back here. Or Zee should have come alone.

"Zee. Babycakes!" A bright male voice rang like a bell across the room, and the demon who strutted over flung his arms wide, then hauled Zee into a bear hug. He wasn't tall, but he was heavy, and wrapped in studded leather under a fluffy blue gown. Since he only had the one spiraling horn, I figured he was Ramone.

"Ram!" Zee grabbed his friend's shoulders and rattled him. "Fuck, you smell like a hundred hoes."

Ramone preened. "Busy night, until I heard you were here. Gotta drop everything for the best cocksucker in town." He propped his ass on a barstool, took out a pink vape, and puffed. "You payin' for this little meet cute or am I off the clock?"

"Need to fuck up a vampire, you in?" Zee said, without fanfare.

Ramone laughed. "Depends. Is there actual fucking involved, or—"

"Just good, ol' fashioned unaliving."

"Fuck, yeah, I'm in. This your idea, all-American beach boy?" Ramone waved the vape at me.

"My name's Adam, and yes."

"Ramone's a good friend," Zee explained, then asked Ramone, "Is Cherise around? We could use her knives on this."

Ram's smile twitched. "She's uh . . . not working." He called Ben over and ordered a drink.

"Not working?" Zee leaned an arm on the bar. "What did *he* fucking do?"

Ramone screwed up his nose and gave his head a shake, ruffling his black hair around his single horn. His wings, black with painted-on white dots, flicked out, one after the other. "Nothing."

It clearly hadn't been nothing.

They both fell quiet. Ben too. And the atmosphere thickened. I didn't need to be a demon who could read emotions to know something bad had happened to Cherise, and Sebastien had likely been behind it. He clearly had an iron grip on all his staff. There were enough strong demons here to take on Sebastien, so why didn't they?

Zee turned to me. "Is Ramone all we'll need, or should we grab a third?"

Ramone looked over, reading me, as I read him. Physically, he was clearly strong. To hold Baroness Reynard down, we'd need muscle. She wasn't going to lay on her back, like Reynard had under Zee's arm. "We could use another, I guess."

Zee cleared his throat and eyed the crowd. "If it's strength we're going for, then Abe is your best bet."

"The wolf shifter who groped you?"

"He's not all that bad. Just drunk—and grabby," Zee smirked. "Besides, he'll kill for a blow job."

I didn't want him to have to do that. All of *that* was supposed to be over. "I don't like it, Zee."

"Kitten, is there anything about this shit-show of a side-life you do like?"

"It's not . . . I just . . ." Now it was my turn to huff into my drink.

"Did you forget to check your morals at the door, honeypie?" Ramone asked. Tired resignation sparkled in his eyes. I'd known what I was walking into. I hadn't expected it to hurt my heart though.

"Well, fucking hallelujah, the prodigal son returns!" Sebastien's voice swept through the room like an oil-slick tidal wave. The sound crawled down the back of my neck, trying to slither under my skin.

The Razoredge's boss glided over, wearing a dapper all-cream suit, buttoned up and precise. He'd braided his white hair into a second tail, while his actual tail glinted with studded diamonds, and his jagged demon wings sparkled with silver rings.

Ben quickly made himself scarce. Zee tensed, and Ramone sat very still, except for drawing on his vape, resigned to his fate.

"If it isn't the stupid little human in *my* kingdom," Sebastien drawled. "And look, he dragged my whore back."

"We're done here," Zee said. He tried to move from the bar, but Seb caught his arm, and hauled him close.

"Done with what?" Seb grinned.

"Nothing," Zee said, trying to shake himself free. But Seb clung on.

He leaned in, mouth parting, and brushed the tip of his tongue over Zee's lips. "You come snaking back here and think to recruit *my* talent? Did you forget I'm always watching?" He nodded toward the back of the bar.

I took me a few seconds to find it, but among the bottles, a small black camera blinked, observing everything. Had he caught our conversation about murdering vampires? Zee's flicker of a glance danced to me and back to Seb's face, where his boss's smile grew. His tail lay limp behind him, not moving at all, and his wings hung low. Defeat. Resignation.

I'd never seen him so beaten. And I *hated* it.

I put my drink down and twisted on the stool. "Let him go."

Seb blinked. Then laughed in Zee's face. "Isn't he adorable. Do you need your pet to talk for you, Zodiac?"

"Adam, just go," Zee mumbled.

"Not without you."

Ramone's hand came down on my shoulder, but I shook it off. "Sebastien, let him go. He's coming home with me."

"Home?" Sebastien laughed, and yanked Zee around, dragging him by the arm. "You seem to be confused. His home is right here. *With me.*" He growled so deeply, its rumble trembled in my chest.

"Adam—" Zee began. Sebastien pulled Zee against his chest, and slammed a kiss onto his mouth.

I couldn't do anything. Couldn't stop Sebastien. Didn't want to watch him shove his tongue down Zee's throat, and Zee behave as though it was all he deserved.

Sebastien withdrew, licking his lips.

Zee's eyes were downcast, his whole body smaller. *Crushed.*

I couldn't stay quiet a second longer. "You have no right—"

Sebastien lunged, but pulled up short. The air crackled in the inch of space left between us. I lifted my chin and held his gaze. "I have *every* right. Now fuck off, while Zodiac and I get vigorously reacquainted."

"Zee?"

"Go, Adam," he mumbled, his wings so low they dragged

on the sticky floor.

"But—"

"Fucking go!" he roared. Then tore his arm from Sebastien's hold, and marched toward the side door from which Sebastien had entered.

Sebastien smirked. "Didn't I say he'd be back?" He thrust out his chest, flicked his wings back, and bent down so we glared, eye to eye. "I'm going to fuck him extra hard, especially for you. Oh, wait? What's that I taste . . . ?" Sebastien zeroed in on my face, staring into my eyes. "Do you have *feeeeeelings* for Zodiac?"

I flinched, briefly dropping my gaze, then stared right back. But it was too late.

"Fuck me, you do! Oh, you poor little human. He got you good." Sebastien pinched my chin between his finger and thumb. "Do you know how many people think they love Zodiac? You're a drop in the ocean, babe." Sebastien's laugh ran over me like liquid. "This must hurt, since you want him, but to me, he's just *meat* to *fuck*." On the emphasis, he rolled his tongue, lips apart, enjoying the taste of those words. "While I own him, he will never be free to be yours. And I will never let him go."

Rage boiled over.

I tore my chin free and swung for his too-pretty face.

Ramone caught my wrist, holding me back.

Sebastien's eyes widened. "Don't wait up." He laughed, spun, and vanished through the door after Zee, slamming it closed behind him. I glared at that door, wishing I could burn through it, burn this whole place to the ground. Maybe the whole world too.

Ramone let go of my wrist and backed off. "I'll see you get out of Demontown safely."

"Don't bother. I'm staying."

"Zee won't want that."

My heart sank. It was all too easy to imagine the horrible things Sebastien was about to do to Zee—my friend. He clearly hadn't wanted go with him, but was used to it. It would be easier to give in to a horrible bully like Sebastien than fight him every day.

"If it's any consolation, Zee's a pro. Been working Seb's moods for years. He'll get it done."

"That does not help." My voice creaked through clenched teeth.

The music thumped against the inside of my skull, and whatever drink I'd been served soured my insides. I didn't want to go, but Ramone and Zee were right. There was no use in me staying, while upstairs they . . . I closed my eyes and squeezed my hands into fists. Squeezed them so tight I trembled. And then, with a breath, I sighed it out.

This could not touch me.

I already had too much . . .

I had to leave. Go. Just like Zee had said.

"We'll be in touch with the details," I told Ramone.

"I look forward to it, babycakes." He mustered a sad smile.

I left Razorsedge, keeping my head down. The crowds lining up to get into bars shifted out of my way, watching me pass, as though sensing I was bait better left alone. I made it almost to the district limits, then pulled up short.

I could go back to the hotel, or . . . not? Glancing over my shoulder, the revelry of Demontown beckoned, its neon lights trying to lure in unsuspecting humans for a wild night some would not survive.

But I was no unsuspecting human.

I turned on my heel, and strode back the way I'd come. But this time, I walked deeper into the darkness, where the streetlights had been smashed and the shadows were thick.

A smile tucked into my cheek. I'd show them bait . . .

CHAPTER 7

"ADAM, DARLING, WHAT ARE YOU DOING?" Madame Matase appeared on the garden path behind me. She might have been there a while, but I'd been engrossed in planting.

On my knees, in the newly dug flower beds, I looked up and brushed the bangs from my eyes. She looked nice, in a flower-print black dress, her wavy black hair pinned back from her kind face. "The garden was neglected, so I fixed it up." I gestured at the rows of happy flowers in their beds.

She blinked a little too long at me, then smiled at the flowers. "You did all this since last night?"

"Started it last night, then bought some flowers when the store opened this morning." I brushed mud from my slacks, smearing more soil across my thighs. My hands were coated, my nails black. I was fairly certain I had mud in my hair too. After getting back from Demontown, I'd needed to do something wholesome, and the neglected garden had been the first thing I'd seen.

"It's going to rain. Come inside." She seemed worried, but she didn't need to be.

"Good, flowers like rain."

"Darling." She looked at me oddly, studying my face. Her eyebrows pinched, but her eyes stayed kind. "Are you alright?"

"Fine. Yes. I am fine. Everything is fine." Why wouldn't I be fine? It wasn't as though my demon, sometimes lover had been ordered to sleep with his ex-boss, and had likely had to endure unspeakable things, and I hadn't been able to stop it. Nor was it as though a powerful sorcerer was still out there, thinking up all the ways he could ruin my last chance at a free life. Or that a shady vampire's wife wanted my head on a plate, because I was promised to her queen. Why would I be anything but fine?

"Good, because you must look after yourself. This hotel needs you." She brushed dirt from my stained T-shirt. "We need you."

I smiled at her concern, and followed her into the lobby. Sunlight streamed in through the windows, highlighting all the scuffs on the floor, the faded paint and tattered furniture. There was still so much to do.

"Adam, I've been meaning to ask," she began, settling behind the reception desk. "A few nights ago, the wards behaved strangely. Do you have any idea why?"

"Oh?" I blinked at Madame Matase, and rubbed my forehead. Tiredness muffled my thoughts. I shouldn't have stayed out in Demontown. Shouldn't have indulged in *things*.

"Yes, and well, the wards *expanded*." She whispered the last part and glanced around us, checking nobody heard.

"They expanded?"

"They grew, yes. As skilled as I am, my reach only goes so far. But the wards have grown."

"I didn't know wards could do that?"

"It rather depends on the power of the person crafting them. As I said, I'm adequate, but not without my limits."

"Oh well, bigger wards is no bad thing, I guess."

"Except, they've expanded beyond the hotel grounds." She kept her voice low again.

"How far?" I whispered.

"Just a short way, onto the sidewalk, and the road. They can't be seen, so it's not as though anyone is going to notice. But as I didn't craft that, I thought you should know. It's rather . . . unusual."

"What would cause it?"

"Another ward weaver with intimate knowledge of my patterns. But as we don't have any guests who know me, I doubt it's that. Or a power surge. Sometimes powerful Lost Ones exude energy, in certain circumstances, that can boost wards."

"Circumstances like . . . ?"

"High pressure situations, threats, something emotional. It would take something powerful though."

Emotional like . . . maybe . . . having drunk sex on the roof with a demon lover? "Do we have any guests with that level of power?" I asked, hoping I was wrong. We didn't technically note a guest's particular ability when they arrived, but Madame Matase was very good at assessing any Lost Ones, especially those who might be *difficult*.

"None I am aware of."

"Well, we do have a shadowbeast in the attic." It was probably Shadow.

"The wards could have responded to a being from between the veil, I suppose. But they would usually shrink back to their normal size again, after whatever event that had caused them to expand had passed."

"And they haven't?"

"No."

"Well, as it's not harming anyone, I don't think we need to worry. Thank you for bringing it to my attention. I'm going to get cleaned up." I'd think on it later, when my head wasn't foggy. I should check in on Shadow too, and make sure they were content in their new space.

Breakfast was being served in the restaurant, and the lounge thrummed with guests readying for their day sightseeing in San Francisco. The hotel appeared to be ticking along nicely without my assistance. And so, traipsing mud through the hotel, I took the stairs—avoiding the busy elevator—but hesitated on my floor, with Zee's room on the next floor up.

What if I knocked at his door and he wasn't in? What if he *was*, and I had to see the marks on his wrists and neck again?

I couldn't . . . I just couldn't. Not with my head so messy. I'd say or do something I couldn't take back.

In my room, I showered and dressed, then donned my host's smile to venture into the day. What remained of the morning passed without incident, giving me time to fall back into my role, until Reynard emerged from his room in the late afternoon. He found me in the lounge, replacing complimentary books on their shelves.

He drew closer, bid me a good afternoon, and picked up a copy of the *Wilson's Guide*.

"I have a plan for your problem," I told him.

He slid the guide back among the other books. "I'm listening."

"An ambush. I'm the bait."

He blinked slowly and considered his reply, either because he didn't like it and was thinking of a way to argue with me, or because he hadn't expected me to offer myself up so readily. "You've seen how fast she is."

I had. She was, admittedly, faster than I could track. "I don't think she'll kill me. She wants me alive."

"Agreed. But she could render you helpless as fast as—" He snapped his fingers.

"I'm not so easy to *render helpless.*"

A beat passed, then another. "Indeed."

"I will be bringing along some assistance," I added, before he could ask something silly. Like why I thought I could stand off against a vampire when I was merely a human with no special talents or abilities whatsoever. None. "You just need to contact your wife and tell her we're going on a date, during which, you'll deliver me on a silver platter."

"This is . . . I'm uncomfortable with the risk. If something were to happen to you, I'd never forgive myself."

"And Zee will pull your spine out through your, uh . . ." I trailed off, and cleared my throat. Reynard's eyes widened. "Well, you catch my meaning. I won't get hurt. We'll have plenty of backup, and she'll be walking into an ambush. If anything goes wrong, we have the man—demonpower to escape."

"Demons?" Reynard grumbled.

"Who did you expect me to ask for help?"

"Are they trustworthy?"

"I don't really know them, but Zee does, and he would never go along with this if he thought there was a risk to me, so we're good." He frowned, clearly unhappy with the situation. "You've tried everything else, and you've failed, so this is what we've got."

He folded his arms and leaned against the bookcase. "I remain unconvinced."

"Or you walk out of here and lose your head."

He winced. "If this ambush fails, I'll lose my head regardless. Perhaps my demise is what the demon wants? Have you considered that?"

I hadn't, and he wasn't wrong. Zee could absolutely turn this around on Reynard. He'd broadcast his opinion of Reynard loud and clear. "It is a risk for you, but I trust him. Do you trust me?"

"I do," he admitted. "More than is logical for someone I've just met."

"Ah, Mr. Vex! There you are," a man squawked. I recognized the voice, but it took me a few seconds to place it. "I asked at reception," he said, hurrying over. "But they didn't seem to know how to find you." Detective Somers inserted himself into our private conversation and flashed his SFPD badge.

A glimmer of irritation cut like a knife through Reynard's gaze, but his rapid smile banished it. "Detective," he purred.

Somers, a bulky man, with a thick neck and narrow-set eyes, pointed his pen at Reynard. "You're that tech guy, right? I've seen you on the news."

"I am the *tech guy*, yes. Charmed, I'm sure. Is there something I can help you with?"

"Ah, not you. I'm here for Mr. Vex. I'd like to ask you some questions Mr. Vex."

"Wonderful," I beamed. "But I'm in the middle—"

"Have you seen your business partner . . . *Zodiac,* isn't it?"

He knew very well what Zodiac's name was. "Not this morning, why?"

"Well, funny thing. Like I said before, Demontown and Lost Ones ain't my remit, but you see, your partner makes quite the impression wherever he goes. Hard to miss, right? And he was sighted in Demontown last night."

Where was this irritating man going with this? "Yes, he is a demon, so—"

"That's what I thought, but see, last night, two more demon bodies were found, slaughtered . . . like before. And I got to thinking. Isn't it strange how Zodiac goes back to Demontown, and the next morning there are dead demons being scraped off the ground? Don't you think that's strange?"

Reynard cleared his throat. "Far be it from me to tell you

how to do your job, Detective, but it's Demontown. I'd hazard a guess, finding a few dead demons is just another night there, no?"

"Yeah, you see, the Supe Feds think that too, so they're not looking into it all that hard. What's demons killing demons got to do with the rest of the law-abiding San Franciscan citizens, right? Just so long as they keep it in Demontown, nobody cares." He shrugged, and glanced between us, reading more than his casual glances let on.

"I was with him," I said, losing my patience.

"Again? Well isn't that convenient, Mr. Vex?"

I was not in the right frame of mind to deal with Detective Somers. "What do you want?"

"Justice?" he quipped. "The Supe Feds may not be interested in the murders, and I wouldn't normally be either, but it's the manner in which they were killed, see? Lost Ones killing Lost Ones happens every day, but not like this. Whatever killed those first few demons I mentioned . . . and these new murders? Well, it was vicious. It didn't just kill them, it tore them apart. Which is all well and good in Demontown, but what if something powerful enough to take on three demons decides it doesn't want to stay in Demontown?"

"Perhaps those demons deserved it," I said. "Maybe they had cruel intentions, and whatever they hunted turned out not to be the easy prey they'd thought." I caught Reynard's eye. He gave his head an almost imperceptible shake. "I mean . . . or maybe there was more than one killer? I'm not sure what you're implying—"

"You know exactly what I'm implying Adam Vex."

I did. He was trying to frame Zodiac for murders I knew he did not commit, because he was a racist cop who didn't like how a demon porn star was now running a hotel in a quiet, well-respected San Franciscan neighborhood. The truth was a whole lot worse, but it also didn't fit his facts.

"Maybe the Feds should take a closer look?" Somers suggested.

"Do you have any evidence?" I asked.

He swallowed, and glanced between Reynard and me. "It's just a matter of time before he's caught. Make it easier for him. Tell him to hand himself in to the authorities—"

"Well, you're wrong about him, and you should go."

"I'm rarely wrong."

"Shall I escort you to the door, Detective?" Reynard asked, all smiles and kind eyes. But those eyes could bewitch, and the tiniest of shivers running down my spine suggested he might attempt to do exactly that, once outside the reach of the wards.

"No need." Somers smiled, tucking his pen and notepad back into his jacket pocket.

"I insist." Reynard planted a hand on the detective's shoulder and guided him away. I might have felt bad about Reynard using his talents on a human, if that human hadn't been a racist asshole.

While Reynard dealt with the detective, I headed up to my room. The moment the elevator doors opened, I caught sight of Zee pacing outside my door. He looked up and a broad grin broke out across his face. That grin made everything alright, and lifted a horrible weight off my shoulders. A weight I hadn't realized I'd been carrying since leaving him at Razorsedge.

"I brought you a gift," he said, showing me the garden ornament cast in the shape of a cat, cradled in the crook of his arm.

"Zee, you don't need to buy me gifts."

"Pfft, it was sitting in someone's yard. Unwanted and alone."

That was generally what garden ornaments did. "Did you steal it?"

"I fucking liberated it." He strutted into my room and slammed the stone cat down on my dresser, depositing bits of grass and moss. "Now it's yours."

At least we now had a garden for it to go in. Although, I was tempted to try and get it back to its owner before I adopted it into my cat-figurine family.

He looked good in an understated—for him—purple suit jacket, purple and black tartan kilt, plus lace-up knee-high boots with chonky heels. There didn't appear to be any signs of Sebastien having done *things* to him, but Zee could hide minor imperfections, like bruises.

"How are you?" I asked, trying to make it sound casual.

His wings pricked. "Fucking great, Adam. Just fucking great. How are *you*?"

Wow. This was not a good start. It was probably best to clear the air before I updated him on the murder-a-vampire plan. "Look, I'm sorry—"

"Don't." He turned on his heel, wings flaring, tail knotting. "Don't say anything. Don't mention anything. Don't look at me like you are right now. That life stays there." He threw a hand at the window. "And this one . . ." He pointed at the floor. "This one is you and me, right here. It stays here, where that—" His voice quivered, and I almost went to him, but he swept a hand through his hair, ruffling the purple and black locks around his horns, and sighed through his nose. "Here is where that shit is not fucking welcome. What happens in Demontown stays in Demontown."

If that was what he wanted, I had no right or claim to persuade him otherwise. "Alright."

He sniffed, lifted his chin, flung a smile onto his face, and flopped into my dresser chair. "Al-fucking-right then. I have news. Abe is in."

And I wasn't going to ask how he'd bribed the lupine

shifter into killing a vampire, when I already suspected I knew the answer.

"That makes you"—he counted on his fingers—"me, Abe, Ramone, and Vampire Daddy. Abe is worth, like, three fucking demons when he gets his wolf on. It's some impressive, completely unhinged, fucked-up, rabid Cujo shit. He'll chew up that vampire hoe like she's a squeaky toy."

I told him how Reynard was going to lure her in by taking me to dinner a second time, which he grumbled about, but was on board. Now all we needed was a location that accepted Lost Ones, and didn't look like a trap. Somewhere Reynard was likely to invite me, but also didn't mind getting blood on their tablecloths.

All the restaurants Zee knew had waist-height holes in their restroom cubicles.

We needed somewhere classy—somewhere convincing.

Somewhere without wards.

CHAPTER 8

REYNARD WAS GOING to take me *dancing*.

Swing, apparently. Before we left the hotel, Zee began to impart some very important and sexually explicit rules about group sharing, forcing Reynard to clarify that swing was not, in fact, swing*ers*, but a style of music.

We left Zee on the porch, his eyes narrowed on Reynard and tail flicking. He'd meet us at the club once he'd rallied the others.

Reynard settled into the back seat of a new car, next to me, and off we went. "Are you quite sure the demon does not have designs on my demise?"

"You can say his name, you know? Make him more real and less of an object to hate."

Reynard sat very still, then breathed in and looked over. "Are you quite sure *Zodiac* does not intend this ambush for me?"

"I'm sure. There, see? Saying his name didn't hurt." I grinned and leaned back into the soft leather seats. "You're doing great. This is great. Dancing is great."

He continued to stare. "Are you nervous, Adam?"

I stroked my sweaty palms on my thighs and chuckled. "No."

After waiting a beat, he said, "This will not be like our last dinner."

No, because at the end of this one, the world would have one less vampire in it, and Baron Reynard would be missing his baroness. My heart thumped. Everything was going to be super fine!

"Adam, look at me."

I did, and blinked through a blur brought on by too much oxygen. Reynard reached inside his jacket and produced a square piece of paper. He proceeded to fold the paper back and forth, making tight little creases. Not an easy thing to do in a moving car, but he managed it, smoothing it out over his thigh. And when he was done, he opened his hand, and on his palm sat a paper swan.

"A gift."

I picked it up, afraid to crush the fragile, beautiful thing.

"Don't you feel better?" he asked.

I'd stopped hyperventilating, so that was something. "Thank you." I did feel better. *Suspiciously* better. Eyes narrowed, I asked, "Did you do something with this swan?"

"Do what?"

"I don't know, ward it maybe?" I eyed the little swan. The angles were perfect. Of course they were. Reynard did not suffer messy lines. But who took a piece of paper from their jacket, with no creases, and whipped up a perfect swan like that, without some kind of power behind it?

He laughed so softly it was almost soundless in the muffled car. "Adam, sometimes a paper swan is just a paper swan."

I laughed a little too. He was right. Not everything had to be a trap. Sometimes a paper swan was just a paper swan. A warm, genuine smile settled on my lips. "Thank you."

"You're welcome. Despite the motives behind this evening, I hope you'll enjoy the company."

"I'm sure I will."

Well, this was . . . nice. Kind of like an actual date. Which this wasn't. This *not*-date *was* a trap, just not designed for me.

Reynard's driver dropped us outside a vibrant waterside venue. Its big windows framed a glistening view of the glossy bar inside, with lots of sparkly, well-dressed people around polished tables. I sensed rather than saw Lost Ones among the crowd, since there were a lot of people here. Reynard led me through the front door, and into the main bar area filled with bubbling chatter. Further toward the back, a live band played an upbeat number, tempting people onto the dance floor. Some clearly knew how to dance, while others loitered at the edges, not as certain. But the party atmosphere had infected my mood, and had my toe tapping.

Reynard offered to buy me a drink, and the human bartender delivered our order without arguing, or swearing, or trying to poison us, or get us high.

"Quite the treat, receiving the drinks we ordered," Reynard commented, leaning against the bar.

"I was thinking the same."

We chinked glasses and sipped. His eyes dazzled under the bar lighting. His smile gleamed too. His classy suit combined with his long black hair, loose down his back, drew some glances. He had to be one of the most handsome people here. Many probably recognized him too.

"Tom Collins has other talents though," I said, leaning next to him, and casually glancing around the bar. There were a lot of people here. Reynard had suggested it would be a good place for an ambush, but I hadn't expected it to be so busy.

"Such as?"

"He's a good listener."

"Do you tell him your secrets?" Reynard asked, with a mischievous lilt to his voice.

"Some," I teased. Reynard had been paying attention over the two weeks since we'd met. Like at the meeting at Cain Tower—during which he'd been thrown through a window— where Gideon Cain had revealed how I wore illegal glamor. Reynard could not have missed that. Humans did not wear glamor. But he hadn't asked *what* I was. He'd claimed he had no interest in my secrets, just in staying under our roof to avoid his family. But he'd also neglected to mention that he'd intended to wrap me up as a gift to his queen—and how he had a wife. So . . .

I couldn't afford to forget his original motives, or why we were here, even if he did look good enough to devour.

"I assume you dance?" I asked, after watching the collection of people dancing to the upbeat, jazzy music.

"I do. Do you?"

"I can . . . but haven't done, in a long time."

"Why is that?"

"Oh, you know. Busy." *Busy hiding . . .*

"What did you do before investing in the hotel, Adam?"

I smiled, and sipped my drink. I wasn't so relaxed that he'd be teasing any answers out of me.

"Ah yes, of course." His smile grew. "You're a secretive individual. I respect that."

"Thank you. It's for the best."

He twisted, leaning back against the bar, and side-eyed me. "Still, I can't pretend not to be intrigued."

"You can be intrigued all you like, Lord Reynard."

"What do I have to do, for you to address me as Victor?"

I had called him Victor once, when I'd been angry at him. I wasn't entirely sure we were there yet. Zee was right about one thing, Reynard clearly had his own motives for entering our lives. And not all of those would align with ours. Some distance between us was a good, healthy thing. Although, right now, there wasn't much physical distance. The bustling crowd had pushed us closer. My elbow brushed his, and as he didn't flinch away, I pretended not to notice and left it there.

"I thought we were friends?" he asked, leaning closer, since the music had gotten louder.

"We were, before I learned about your plot to gift me to your queen."

"Ah, yes, kidnapping does put a negative spin on things."

"Tell me about your queen. If you were going to gift me, then she must be this side of the veil, no? But there's been no mention of her in four years. I doubt a vampire queen could hide . . ." I trailed off, straying into uncomfortable territory.

"I'm not at liberty to say." He broke our eye contact and gazed at the dance floor.

Were the vampires up to something? It certainly wasn't any of my business what vampires did. And if their queen was here, in hiding, I definitely had no right to judge.

"Shall we dance?" he asked, changing the subject.

I winced, and waggled my half-finished drink. "Maybe after some warming up?"

Reynard shrugged off his jacket, rested it over the bar, and unbuttoned his cuffs—and my brain *went there*. Those quick fingers unclipped his cufflinks, then he rolled up his sleeves, exposing strong forearms that I hadn't had around me nearly enough. "Do you mind if I do?"

"Do what?"

"Dance?"

"Oh, please, go ahead." Yes, I would definitely be watching *that*. He smiled and was gone, consumed briefly by the crowd.

He always seemed so reserved—formal, strict—that I

wasn't entirely sure what I was about to witness. If he dad danced, and Zee missed it, my demon would be devastated. Then, I spotted him on the dance floor, shaking out his hands, and since this was a swing dance club, he began to walk on the spot. It should have looked like dad dancing—walking in time with the beat—but he rocked his hips, adding a spicy sashay to his movement that he had no right being so good at. Then came the triple stepping and kick ball change, and those long, lean legs did their *thang*. I could already hear Zee's explicit comments about having those legs wrapped around me.

By the stars, of course he could dance. He'd had a thousand years to practice.

A space had opened around him, people sensing that maybe they should move away from the man who made them all look like amateurs. Then a woman stepped in, clearly talented, and the pair of them began to jive the Charleston step, with skips and kicking and— mercy was it hot in here?

Reynard turned his partner. She spun, her dress flared, and they made the perfect couple.

I definitely was not jealous. At all.

I also wasn't here to dance, or have fun. This was strictly the business of murdering.

At least *he* was having fun.

I downed my drink and ordered another.

Was there anything he wasn't good at? Why couldn't he be an ugly, mean-spirited, horrible, untalented, bunny-boiling nosferatu? He'd have been so much easier to hate. No, he had to be gorgeous, charming, smart, and sexy, with a tiny side order of psycho.

I could *hear* Zee's smirk, and how he'd tell me to get up close and personal with Vampire Daddy already, just so long as I kept my wits about me. But that was Zee. Sex was his answer to everything.

I kinda just wanted to dance . . .

Okay. Fine.

I downed the second drink, shrugged off my jacket, then handed both jackets to the bartender to watch for us. Reynard was still causing a stir on the dance floor with his lovely partner, who was probably a very nice person, but was absolutely dancing with *my* not-date and needed to back off.

Reynard saw me approach, spun his girl into his arms, whispered in her ear, and she sashayed off. The rest of the partners continued to dance, while Reynard stopped and held out a hand, beckoning me forward.

He'd garnered an audience, too.

Half of me screamed, to *run and hide*. But the other half, the half that controlled my hips and heart, was already dancing. I stepped in, took his hand, and glided into the dance, remarkably slotting in right where his lady had left off. The jazz took control of my body, while Reynard set the tone. Within a few beats, I'd lost myself to the music, and Reynard. We had a few mishaps, but it wasn't long before we synced. Then there was no stopping us. We jauntily danced—wrists bent, hips swinging, shoulders rocking, kicks flying.

I'd never seen him smile like it.

Soon, we had almost the entire dance floor, and a crowd clapping us on, but I didn't see any of it. I saw only Reynard, and felt only the beat of the music thumping through my veins.

The music ended, and rapturous applause washed over us in a wave. We were expected to bow, but I had Reynard's hands in mine, and I stared into his eyes. We panted hard, sweat glistened, faces flushed.

Reynard broke the gaze first, by swallowing and blinking away. I came back into the moment, suddenly aware we were not alone, or horizontal and wrapped in each other's arms. The crowd was still clapping. We bowed to the cheers.

Reynard kept his hand in mine, and as we rose, he pulled me from the club, out a back door, and onto a huge outdoor terrace with the glistening bay surrounding us. Most everyone was inside, probably due to the cold night air.

We leaned on the rail. Water lapped at the bank beneath the deck, and the city hummed in the distance.

I shivered, but not from cold. Adrenaline surged, my whole body ablaze. I'd rarely felt so . . . alive.

Reynard turned to face me and stepped close, as close as when we'd been dancing. His fingers flicked hair back from my sweaty cheek, and then his eyes were pulling me in, his lips luring me closer. It felt right, when his mouth skimmed mine. Electric shivers skittered down my back, and all at once I was in his arms, mouth on his, teasing his lips apart. The kiss lit me up, like our dancing had, and brought me to life. Made my body sing with need. Made me . . . free. He kissed as though we were precious, as though this moment should be savored. His lips teased, as though I was the most valuable thing in all the worlds, and my wounded heart fluttered to life.

"Bravo!" Baroness Reynard's slow clap cracked the quiet, and we lurched apart—breathless, ablaze. "Well this explains *so much*."

Caught making out with her husband. Oops.

"Wife," Reynard snarled.

"Husband," she purred back.

A blood-red wool coat fell from her shoulders. She approached, weaving through the empty tables and chairs, coat flaring like a cloak. "Well, at least you upheld your end of the deal, husband dear. Finally."

"W-What?" I stammered, after a buffering delay, as my brain tried to backpedal from its brief interlude of thinking from my dick. I was supposed to be shocked she was here. "What have you done?" I demanded of Reynard, in a terrible attempt at dramatic acting. We had a script, but the murderous glare and chesty growl, directed at his wife, suggested he wasn't in the mood to recite it.

I glanced at the dark, rippling waters to my left, and the waterside banks behind his wife's approach. Any moment now . . . *C'mon, Zee . . .*

The baroness stopped a table's length from us, and dragged her unimpressed glare over me. "I don't know what you see in this little lamb. I didn't believe you could get any more pathetic, but dating your food is a new low, husband. It's as though I don't even know you."

"Because you never did." His growl minced the words, made them menacing.

"Pfft." She flicked her wrist. "Come along quietly now, little lamb." She extended her hand, expecting me to take it.

"I'm not going anywhere with you."

"Come now. For all my husband's posturing, he cannot protect you—not without losing his head. So do be a dear and surrender. You can beg for your life in the car."

Reynard stepped between us. "You need to leave, Rosanna. Now. Before it's too late for you."

Her laugh tinkled across the water. "What are you going to do, darling? Set me on fire? Chop me into tiny pieces? You haven't tried crucifixion in a few hundred years. Perhaps that'll work this time? Hm? Do you remember the time you attempted to curse me? Ah, marital bliss. You made a promise, Victor, you keep it. Those are the rules. Be grateful this will go no further. You!" She snapped her fingers at me. "Come. Now."

Zee . . . Where are you?

What if he'd been waylaid? What if he couldn't make it? What if it was just Reynard and me?

What if Zee did intend to trap Reynard too?

"Lamb, if you do not come, your lover—my husband—

will die. While I could not care less, you appear to have feelings for the wretched failure of a man. Do you want him to die because of you? Frankly, even as the wet lettuce he is, his life is worth ten times yours, so stop wasting everyone's time and accept your fate."

Nobody was around, no witnesses. I had certain abilities I could potentially wield, but not without Reynard seeing. He already knew too much. If I could get her alone, somewhere private, away from Reynard, then there was a chance the Baroness Reynard and I could settle this.

"All right."

Reynard growled. "Adam—"

"It's fine. She's right. I have to go. Or you . . . well . . . you know."

"I refuse." He turned to face me, blocking the route to his wife.

"It's not for you to refuse."

"Adam, you can't go." His eyes widened with a hint of panic. "No life is worth more than mine, certainly not yours."

How could I tell him everything was going to be fine, without *telling* him everything was going to be fine? "Like I said, *it's fine*."

"If you kiss again, I might vomit," Baroness Reynard said. "Really, it's like the master kissing his dog. Viccy, I swear, if there's a new low, you find it every time—"

A blood-curdling howl tore through the night, reverberating across the bay, the source impossible to pin down.

Backup had arrived. Finally.

"Speaking of dogs." I side-stepped Reynard and leveled my glare at the baroness. Her fine eyes narrowed, suspicion sinking in. She'd been cut up, set ablaze, crucified, and cursed. But had she been attacked by a werewolf, a couple of aggressive sex demons, her furious husband, and me all at once?

She sneered at Reynard, and echoed my earlier sentiment, when she said, "What have you done?" But unlike my acting, her outrage was real.

Baroness Reynard's evening was about to take a turn for the worse.

CHAPTER 9

AN ENORMOUS BLUR of grey thundered behind Baroness Reynard—how I imagined a charging bear might look, if a bear had a long muzzle full of jagged, vicious teeth, and blazing red eyes. She didn't see it, but Reynard did. He gallantly manhandled me behind him, trying to keep me safe, but the werewolf wasn't here for us.

Abe sprang off muscular back legs and slammed into the baroness, driving her face first into the deck. Tables and chairs flew like skittles. Abe locked his jaws around her waist and shook, rattling the baroness like a doll. Splashes of blood and bits of coat rained. It was horrific, but also . . . beautiful. Like watching the poetry of karma in action.

Did I say beautiful? Not that. Definitely horrific. Brutal. Terrible, really.

Abe yelped, spat the baroness from his mouth, and cowered, raising his paw.

Uh oh.

The baroness jerked and twitched, rising to her feet, dislocated limbs locking back into their sockets. She brandished her bloody stiletto shoe—the weapon she'd used on Abe. Her hair was a ragged mess, her face all shredded from its trip along the deck.

"You've never looked better, dear," Reynard purred, his voice thick with satisfaction. And maybe some lust too. Bloody violence was probably right up a vampire's kink street, as Zee would say. Where *was* Zee?

"You bitch!" Baroness Reynard screeched at her husband. "You've ruined another coat!"

A heavy demon—not Zee—dropped out of the sky like a bomb, slammed into her, and drove her through the timber deck in an explosion of splinters.

Reynard turned to me, silver eyes ablaze. "Stay here. Stay out of trouble. Do not get involved."

"Sure." I thrust my hands into my pants pockets, more than happy not to flex abilities that I definitely did not have.

I righted a nearby chair and dropped into it. A few screams had erupted inside the bar, now its customers had noticed the carnage.

The only thing missing, for me to truly enjoy the show, was popcorn.

Reynard's wife screamed. Then everything fell quiet for a bit, allowing the sound of distant sirens to leak in. A pale, bloody hand reached up through the hole in the deck. Then a second, followed by a mass of knotted hair, and Baroness Reynard came crawling out of the hole like a witch from a Korean horror movie.

The next demon who dropped out of the sky was one I knew well.

Zee landed hard on her wrists, stabbing his bootheels through her flesh, pinning her to the deck. His tail lashed like a whip, then swooshed around and cinched around her neck. His jagged wings flared behind him in a glorious display of demon magnificence.

He knelt, and stroked a nail down her choking, scarlet

face. "Nobody *hurts* Adam, wench. Also, your fashion sense is so painful, I'll be glad to put you out of your obvious misery. *You're welcome.*" His voice had dropped an octave, morphing into auditory danger.

She wasn't done, though. She twisted her head, and sank her fangs into Zee's tail. He let out a cry and reeled, stumbling backward, but also freeing up her arms. She flew at him, hitting him like a wrecking ball. I jerked from the chair, protective instincts kicking in. Nobody touched Zee!

"Don't!" Reynard snarled, marching toward the scrapping pair. "We've got this." Behind him, Ramone moved up, and behind *him*, limped Abe.

The group was impressive, and together they made it clear —Baroness Reynard would not survive this encounter.

I lowered myself back into the chair. As it happened, this was turning out to be quite the date.

But the wailing sirens suggested they needed to hurry it along.

Cold, hard steel touched my neck, and a smooth, male voice whispered in my ear. "Make a sound, and I'll cut your throat."

I didn't recognize the speaker, but felt his intent. He would execute that threat, and me.

Reynard and Zee were focused on beating the baroness. Abe had her pinned now. Zee had her tied up with his tail, and Reynard was moving in.

I opened my mouth to alert them. The knife cut in, choking me off. Blood dribbled.

"Easy now. Stand, then back up with me."

I stood slowly, careful to keep the blade's edge from digging any deeper. It would be fine. Once the blade was free of my neck, I'd call out.

"Easy . . ." my kidnapper warned.

I backed up toward the edge of the deck, guided by the

stranger's voice, and his touch. If Zee would just look over, he'd see I was in trouble. Any second now, someone would look, and they'd see, and they'd come—

A blow thwunked the back of my head. I blinked, and found myself face down on the deck, head spinning. How had I gotten there—

A second blow stopped all thought, and darkness rushed in.

CHAPTER 10

I HADN'T CONSIDERED that Baroness Reynard might bring her own backup. And now I was tied to a chair, bolted to the floor in a small basement, with the only light spilling in from a tiny barred window. A camera blinked its beady eye at me from the corner of the room.

I was being watched.

Well, this was not the end I'd imagined for what had been —until getting knocked unconscious—an excellent date.

All things considered, it could have been worse. I was alive, so there was that.

Clearly, whoever had taken me didn't want me dead.

Plus, Reynard and Zee would be doing everything to track me down. Probably. Assuming there hadn't been any more surprises, and they'd survived the encounter with the baroness.

What if they hadn't?

No, I had to assume they were fine. Otherwise, things really were worse.

The bolts on the heavy basement door clanged, the door swung open, and a short, unassuming man who appeared to be around my age, clomped down the steps. He wore a suit too—typical vampire attire. Did they all wear suits?

He paced back and forth, then hitched up his trousers at the knee, and crouched. "You vex me, Adam Vex," he said, with a sharp British accent.

I smiled. "You know who I am. Seems only fair I should know your name?"

"Ah yes, introductions. Of course. Seems fair, as you say. Roland Spry."

He spoke as though I should know who he was, and frowned when he didn't get an ah-ha.

"Duke Spry," he clarified.

Ah-ha. A duke. So he was far higher on the vampire nobility chart than a baron. Inferior only to the kings, queens, princes, and princesses. I must have been special, to warrant his personal attention. "A duke? This is clearly a misunderstanding. I'm a nobody. I think you have the wrong man."

He blinked and smiled, clearly not believing a single word, which was a problem.

"I cannot decide if you are as clueless and naïve as you're making out, or if you are, in fact, something of a genius."

I laughed. "Would a genius be tied to this chair?"

He straightened and frowned, pursing his lips, trying to figure me out. "I really wouldn't get involved in these frivolous things, but you see, when a baron takes himself off-grid to flee his responsibilities, it all gets very messy. Airing our dirty laundry in public is unacceptable, and not how this family behaves." He began pacing again, carelessly tossing a few hand gestures out as he spoke. "I would have had it dealt with at a distance, but then, an anonymous note lands on my desk. And do you know what that note says, Mr. Vex?"

I swallowed.

"*Adam Vex is not what he seems*. And I ask myself, where have I heard that name before? Then it hits me. The human hotelier with a death wish. The human we're all laughing at for foolishly housing Lost Ones under his roof. What an idiot. Except . . . you're no fool, Adam." He stopped and looked me dead in the eye. "So I have to ask, what are you?"

I blinked slowly, and glanced at the camera. Still recording. "I don't know what you mean."

He smiled, but it was hollow, sitting there on his lips. "You look at me, and what do you see?" He swept his hands through the air at his sides. "Don't be shy, tell me."

"A man."

He chuckled. "Cute. Now be a little more specific."

"Just a man, erm . . . who wears a nice suit."

"No. Look." He gestured at himself. "What do you see?"

"A human man, around mid-twenties, in a suit, so maybe . . . you work in an office block? I don't know."

"Exactly." Saying the word, revealed his sharp teeth. "I'm a man in a suit. The perfect camouflage. But we both know that's not at all what I am. The Lost Ones have been hunting humans since long before the veil fell. Thousands of years in fact. We slipped back and forth in certain geographical locations, and humans wrote stories about us—warning each other—which of course, nobody believed. We learned to imitate them, so we might better *hunt* them. Why do you wear that human skin, Mr. Vex?"

"Uh." I looked down at myself. "Because it's my skin?"

"No, it isn't."

"Yes it is."

"No, it's really not."

I sighed. "We could do this all day, I guess. Because what you see is what I am."

"We both know that's a lie. You're no fool, so don't treat me as one. You wear powerful glamor."

"Do I?" I sounded surprised.

He laughed, and waggled a finger. "You're very good at

this. Well practiced. You've been hiding for a long time. I'm impressed. I'm also beginning to see why Baron Reynard was interested in you."

"Are you going to get to the point, because the more we talk, the more likely it is my friends will find me. And they'll not be kind. I assume Baroness Reynard is no longer with us, so you know what they're capable of. You should definitely let me go."

"Oh." He chuckled. "They'll never find you in time."

In time for . . . what?

"You see, I was going to let this whole drama play out," Duke Spry continued, hands circling in the air. "The Reynards have been bickering for centuries. It's tiresome, frankly. I was quite happy to let them destroy each other, trying to gift you to our sovereign, but too much around you doesn't add up. Victor Reynard is no fool either, although he acts it so we don't notice him. Why you? Hm? And the anonymous note . . . No, you're not simply a human who happens to manage a run-down hotel. You are a mystery, a riddle, and I will solve you, regardless of how long it takes."

"There's nothing to solve. Really. You're a busy man, and this is a waste of your time. You're going to be disappointed. You should let me go."

He sucked in a deep breath, held it, thinking his answer over, and sighed. "No."

Duke Spry was a problem.

"You have two choices, Mr. Vex. Tell me what you are— avoiding a great deal of anguish—or continue to plead your humanity, and I'll pry the truth out of you, piece by piece." His pupils swelled, and there was that vampire salaciousness. "Think on it. I'll be back for your answer." He marched up the steps and was gone with a clang of bolts.

Well, this was unfortunate.

I eyed the camera again.

Who had told the duke I was not what I seemed? It had to be Gideon Cain, didn't it? The language on the note was the same as that scrawled on my mirror. Gideon was using others to test my defenses, keeping his hands clean and himself at a safe distance. The duke probably didn't know he was a pawn.

I could use that.

But until I knew who was behind that camera, and where the feed went, I couldn't afford to be anything other than human and treat this kerfuffle as just a misunderstanding.

A couple of anonymous guards with orders not to talk, took me on a bathroom break, during which I got a good look at the stone corridor behind the bolted door. Another camera there too. Either the vampires were paranoid, or this place was a prison. The bathroom was nice though, with fluffy towels and sweet-smelling hand soap. But the one small letterbox window wasn't large enough to escape through, which was probably why I was trusted to be alone.

No camera in the bathroom made it a potential weak spot.

Still bound at the wrists, I was marched back to the basement, fixed to the chair, and left there, as the light shifted and hours passed.

The clang of bolts jolted me awake, and down the stairs clomped Duke Spry. An old woman tottered behind him, as round as she was tall, with a nest of gray hair sat on top of her head. Her small eyes, sunken in their sockets, resembled two clumps of coal.

"We found this when we searched you," the duke said, showing me the crumpled paper swan. The poor thing looked like I felt. He placed it on the seat of a chair by the far wall, then returned to me. "Have you decided?"

"I really don't know what you expect me to be? This is just a mishap. Let me go and I won't tell anyone—"

He snapped his fingers. "Work your magic," he told the older lady. "Adam, this is Madame Geraldine. Geraldine is a ward weaver. I assume you know what a ward weaver is, as you have one at your hotel. Geraldine will be helping me out."

I eyed Geraldine warily. She stared back, glare solid as steel.

"The glamor you wear is a type of ward," the duke said, proving he was no fool. "A portable one. They're generally not powerful, and mostly used to hide minor imperfections, or mask one's face temporarily. But yours *is* powerful, and I want to see what it's hiding."

I glared harder at Geraldine, and tried to convey without words how she really did not want to do this. "Do you like cats, Geraldine?"

"What?" she croaked.

"Cats?" I said a bit louder.

"Rats?" She squinted.

"No, cats. Felines. Meow."

"She's a bit hard of hearing," the duke sighed.

"Yes, I like cats," she said.

"Did you know cats see through glamor?" I asked her, almost shouting now.

Geraldine glanced back at the duke.

"Ignore him," the duke barked.

She came closer, raising her hands. Her gnarled fingers began to ripple like spider's legs, *weaving*. Or in this case, *unweaving*.

"I like cats," I told her, trying and failing to hide the quiver in my voice. Whoever Geraldine was, she looked like the kind of weaver who knew what they were doing, and had been doing it for a very long time. There was a chance she might be able to peek inside, and that would be very, very bad.

"I can't keep cats," I said a little quieter, since she was closer now. Her fingers scratched the air between us. "They're afraid of me." She moved in and her coal-like eyes began to glow. Her skill began to pluck at my efforts to remain hidden. "As you should be," I whispered.

Her eyes flicked up, widened. She gasped, then reeled, backpedaling into the duke. He caught her as she collapsed, and the pair crumpled to the floor—the duke, mostly from surprise.

"What the . . ." Duke Spry shoved the no-longer-breathing Madame Geraldine off him, dropping her onto the floor like a sack of potatoes.

"Oh, how terrible." I frowned. "A weak heart, maybe?"

Spry surged to his feet, gaping at the dead ward weaver—then me, still bound to the chair. "You!"

"My hands are literally tied." I jiggled the ties for emphasis. "Too much stress, I think. Did you put her under a lot of pressure? She should have retired years ago."

"You did that!" He thrust a finger at my face, then realized he was as close as she'd been and yanked his hand back, composing himself. "Not to worry, I have another one. I'll go through a whole village of weavers if necessary. I'm getting inside your glamor."

He stormed off—slamming the door—leaving me alone with a dead ward weaver and a crumpled paper swan.

"Sorry." I told Geraldine.

He sent another ward weaver, who also mysteriously suffered a heart attack and died on the spot. The third managed to garble out two words before he fell face first to the floor.

Thankfully, the two words were such a mess the duke had no hope of understanding.

The fourth weaver took a look at me and refused the job. She argued with the duke for a while, but he grew tired of her pleas and killed her himself. That was also my fault, he raged.

After all his efforts had failed, he slumped on the bottom step, head bowed, fingers in his hair.

"I'm just sayin', you should probably let me go."

He flew from that step too fast for me to track, and whipped a backhanded slap across my cheek, setting my face ablaze. I gasped, reeling from the blow I hadn't seen coming. My glamor rippled. Just a little reflexive shimmer. But he saw it.

"You need to learn who it is you are dealing with!" he snapped, sharp fangs gleaming.

I kept my head bowed, kept breathing, listened to my heart pound. If he knew . . . The only thing saving this vampire from a brutal, vicious death, was the camera in the corner. I could smash it, but before I did, footage of my breakout would be captured forever on that little electronic device, and potentially saved off-site for anyone to witness. If that happened, I'd have to run again.

If he knew the ties were as effective around my wrists as paper string—if he knew the truth of me—he'd be on his knees, begging me to spare him.

But he didn't know.

Nobody knew.

Nobody could know.

"I'm just a man," I said, hoping it didn't sound as growly as it had in my head.

He laughed. "All this does is convince me of the opposite." He pointed again. "You're fucked, Adam Vex. Enjoy the view, because you're going to be here for the rest of your days."

He left again, and I slumped in the chair, listening to the sound of his shoes clip away. Reynard's paper swan caught my eye in the gloom. Perhaps he would find me, and perhaps this would have a happy ending, but the real world wasn't a fairytale. Nobody had saved me before.

If I saved myself, the risk was huge.

My gaze fell to the latest dead ward weaver on the floor.

It might just come to that.

CHAPTER 11

"HELLO THERE," the young girl purred, waking me. She couldn't have been any more than eleven years old, with a bouncing blonde ponytail and a smile that meant business. The duke leaned against the back wall, arms crossed, glaring.

A shiver trickled down my spine. Something wasn't right with the smiling girl.

"Hm." She crouched, and rested her chin on a fist. "You're an interesting one."

If she was another ward weaver, I wasn't liking her chances at surviving. I skipped my sleepy-eyed gaze to Spry. She was going to die, just like the others, and this was *his* fault. Not mine. He didn't respond, didn't smile. He was tired of this too.

One of us was going to have to break, and it wouldn't be me.

"Save us the inevitable," the duke drawled. "Tell me what you are."

I breathed in through my nose, and switched my gaze to the girl studying me. "If you do this, you'll end up like the others."

She blinked blue eyes, and said in a chipper voice, "Not me, Mr. Vex. I'm different, see."

I was beginning to sense that, but couldn't tell what she was.

"I'm not going to touch your glamor. Not going to try and take it off, like the others." She stood and began to circle me. Her sneakers scuffed the dusty floor and her ponytail swished. "There's more going on here."

She was right.

The duke's eyes narrowed, turning curious.

Of all the ward weavers who had come before her, she was the only one who had noticed it wasn't just glamor I wore, but something far more dangerous. Something that had gotten them all killed.

She stopped in front of me and crouched again, resting her forearms over her knees. Something about the way she moved, and the glassy sheen in her eyes suggested she wasn't the sweet little girl my senses told me I was looking at.

"You can't remove it, can you?" she said.

My heart raced. "What?"

"You have layers, Mr. Vex. You're a puzzle in a puzzle." She waggled a finger. "You're *cursed*."

My heart flopped.

The duke tensed. "Cursed how?"

The girl continued to stare, her gaze roaming over my face. "You can't remove the glamor," she said to me. "You're trapped inside it, cursed *within* it. You, Mr. Vex, are in chains."

Well, that was a little too close to the truth for my liking. I smiled. "That's ridiculous."

"That's why all the old ward weavers died. Glamor didn't kill them, it's not designed to do that. But a curse did."

"I'm fairly certain it was stress and weak hearts. I didn't kill them."

"No, *you* didn't. The curse did. It's tamper proof. Someone takes a poke and oops, they're dead."

"Can you remove the curse?" the duke asked the girl.

"Not without knowing its engineer." She straightened. "Everyone who tries to unravel that glamor will die. Even you, Duke."

"Well this is most disappointing. I had hoped to find out what he was before—" He cut himself off. "Is there anything you can do?"

"The only way that glamor is coming off, is if the curse is removed first. To do that, I need to know who cursed him, and why."

The duke eyed me. "And you're not likely to tell me who did that, are you, Adam?"

I shrugged. "I don't know what you're talking about. It all sounds like a crazy story to me. If I was cursed, I'd know it."

"He's lying," the girl said.

"I'd gathered that." The duke drew in a deep breath, expanding his chest, and sighed. "I don't have time for all of this. Is there nothing you can do? Any hint at all of what he is? Something more interesting than the meat bag we're looking at?"

"I can tell you that a curse on top of glamor is rare. Whatever is chained inside is powerful. Someone threw everything they had at containing it. Nobody does that unless they're scared of the creature they're chaining." She giggled. "Or punishing it."

I swallowed the hard lump in my throat. This little missy was going on my *Bad People* list.

The duke bowed his head. "All right, thank you, Daisy. That will be all."

"Sure thing." She skipped to the stairs. "Call me back if you need me. I'd like nothing more than to peel the layers off this one."

"I will."

The girl—Daisy—left, taking the chill in the room with her. I still didn't know what she was, but the duke had bowed *to* her, which meant Daisy was not the innocent kid she pretended to be.

"I'm out of time," Duke Spry said, staring down at me. "But you are clearly of importance, and that will have to be enough." He nodded to himself, dragged a hand down his face, and headed for the steps.

"Where does the camera feed go?" I asked.

"The what?" He had his foot on the bottom step, and turned.

"The camera. I'm just curious. Is the footage saved on-site, or is it backed up in the cloud somewhere?"

"I, uh . . . I've no idea. Of all the things you could ask, you ask that?" He left, chuckling to himself at my apparent idiocy. "You really are a riddle, Mr. Vex."

I stared at the paper swan on the little chair. Daisy was right. Nobody threw a curse over a glamor unless they were scared of the thing inside. What she didn't know, was that the origin of the curse was me.

I'd cursed myself.

And I had to get out of here before they figured that out.

At the next bathroom break, the guards shut me in the sumptuous bathroom just like before. No cameras. Just the tiny window, too small to crawl through. But the window was a weak spot, and I could make my own exit.

I snapped the ties and braced against the sink counter. My reflection gazed back—pale, messy, wide-eyed. How long had I been here? Didn't matter. The duke was not going to let me go, and whatever he had planned, it would only get worse.

It was time to make my move.

After shaking out my hands, I climbed onto the toilet and reached for the window. Grabbing the sill, I heaved myself up and peeked outside at an open patch of manicured lawn. The walls of a mansion loomed to the right, windows blazing in the dark. I'd have to be quiet, but nobody was out there. If I was fast, I might be able to escape.

Lowering myself back down, I ran my hands around the weaker section of wall below the window, looking for seams and cracks in the hidden brickwork. Then, spreading my fingers, I shoved. The blocks shifted, plaster cracked. So far so good. But on the second shove, the window popped, shattering.

I winced. Maybe nobody had heard?

"Hey!"

Oh dear. The guards plowed into the bathroom and came at me, hands reaching. No cameras meant I didn't have to hide, just so long as there were no witnesses.

I grabbed the first guard's arm, and flung him against the wall with enough force to knock him out. He dropped, and his mate sprang, going for my neck. He wrapped cold, hard fingers around my throat, and slammed me against the wall, pinning me there.

His murderous glare suggested he'd forgotten the duke wanted me alive.

I scrabbled, trying to shove him off. My lungs burned, screaming for air, and his grip cinched tighter and tighter. He *would* kill me.

I grasped his head in my hands and slammed his ears together, crushing his skull between them. Blood, bits of sticky bone, and squishy brain rained down. I dropped his body, coughing and spluttering, trying to breathe without choking. Something warm and wet coated my lips. I licked at it, then wiped my face clean on my sleeve. There wasn't much

I could do about the splatter coating my shirt and jacket, except hope I wasn't seen.

The guards would be missed if they didn't return soon. I was committed. This was it. Time to escape.

I gave the wall another shove, and a great chunk tumbled out. Cool night air rushed in, tasting like freedom. I scrambled over broken blocks and tumbled onto wet grass, then picked myself up, and crouching low, jogged toward the treeline.

After taking a few strides into the trees, a huge chain-link fence emerged out of the dark. Too high to leap over, it extended left and right, vanishing among the trees. I grabbed at the intertwined metal loops. Sparks rained, and a dart of heat shot up both arms, leaving my fingers tingling. Ah. Warded fencing. I should have expected that.

I'd need to find a hole in the wards—which could take hours—or a gate.

A gate would be closer to the main house. Glancing over my shoulder, I scanned the big house and its lights. If I went back there, the chances of being caught were a great deal higher. I'd try to find a hole first. If the wards were poorly maintained, they might be weaker in places.

But after walking the length of the fence, and stumbling through the brush for what felt like hours, I hadn't found any weakness.

Barking dogs echoed through the night.

That was definitely bad.

I sped up my search, as much as the overgrown bushes allowed, but the barking grew louder, coming closer. They had my scent.

I was going to have to *deal* with them. Muttering a curse, I turned, planted my feet, and waited.

The first hound burst through the brush, barking like a possessed thing. It took it a while—dogs aren't as bright as cats—but the moment it realized its prey was actually a predator it did not want to mess with, the dog dropped to its belly, tail wagging, chops smacking, and whined.

"There it is."

The other dogs raced in, barking, then seeing their alpha on the ground, they hung back, sensing danger first, then *seeing* it. It wasn't long before I had six silly mutts on their bellies, rolling over, tongues lolling. I was embarrassed *for* them. No self respecting predator showed its belly.

But they were adorable, so . . . I scratched the belly of the lead hound, making its leg bounce. It licked blood from my hands. "You're all the best boys. Yes you are. Off you go. Before we get in trouble. Go now, shoo."

They bounded off, and vanished into the dark brush.

"I thought I'd seen it all," Duke Spry said, shoving a sapling out of his way. When the tree bounced back and smacked him in the face, he snapped it in half and tossed the leafy part to the ground with a snarl. "But you're quite the intriguing little toy, aren't you?"

"You should walk away."

"I haven't turned my back on a fight in a thousand years, and I do not intend to start with *you*. Whatever you are."

There were no cameras here, no witnesses. Nobody to tell of the duke's final moments on this earth.

"Who were you going to gift me too? The queen?"

He stopped in a small clearing in front of me, where the dogs had lain. "Indeed. She needs a few more sacrifices, and then we'll be ready. You are a fitting gift."

"No."

"Food doesn't get to choose its fate."

"Food? I thought vampires were smart?" I laughed. "I suppose natural selection doesn't apply if you don't die. You just keep on with your same old ways, never changing, never evolving, never bettering yourselves. As dumb now as you've always been."

"Why would we change, when we're already perfect?" He preened.

"I'm beginning to understand why Victor doesn't much like his family."

"Baron Reynard is nothing," Spry snarled. "He was nothing before the rest of the royal family arrived, and he's less than nothing now."

"*Less* than nothing?" I screwed up my nose.

Spry gestured, palms up. "Y'know, pointless?"

"But you can't have less than nothing. There's nothing, and that's it. It's like saying two hundred percent of something. Two hundred percent doesn't exist."

"Yes it does."

"No, it doesn't."

"It clearly does. *More* than a hundred percent."

"It's an oxymoron."

"*You're* an oxymoron. Shut up!" He stepped closer and pointed a finger at my face. "Now come with me, like the food you are."

"Hm, no." I rolled my shoulders, and took a few steps back toward the fence, loosening up stiff muscles. Sitting in a chair for a few days had left everything feeling tight. "I think I've been quite accommodating, and now it's time I was leaving."

"You can't just leave," he scoffed. "You're my prisoner."

"You can think that, but you're wrong."

"Maybe I was wrong about you. Maybe you're just mad? Mr. Vex, I don't want to force you, but I will. Enough of this nonsense. Come now." He barked those last words, and pointed at the ground in front of him as though I were one of his dogs to be brought to heel.

I lifted my chin. "Make me."

The duke pinched his lips and stomped forward. "Ugh. This is *so* beneath me."

The duke reached for my neck, like most vampires did. I grabbed his arm and spun, then rammed him against the fence, testing a theory. Sure enough, the wards rolled back, letting family members through—and me, currently attached to one. The fence snapped and recoiled, bouncing away, as Spry and I staggered through it.

He snarled, slow to realize he'd been used, and that I was not going to drop to my knees and beg for a treat from my master like the rest of his subjects. He snapped his fangs near my face, and wrestled against my hold. Granted, he was strong. But when I didn't have to pretend, so was I.

He hooked my leg out, dropped me onto my back, and pinned me down, hands around my neck.

Even now, knowing I had to unleash parts of myself, I held back until the very last second.

Spry struck, jabbing his fangs into my shoulder, through my clothes. I cried out, pain flourished, and the glamor began to ripple. Power surged, rolling through me like a tidal wave. Fire and fury filled my head. Rage. So much rage. And fear. A lifetime of fear.

My heart expanded—filling, pumping.

I tore the vampire off, ripping his fangs from my arm, and held him aloft.

Blood dripped from his fangs and down his chin. He paled, dangling like the doll he was, and despite him seeing only pieces of my truth, it was enough for his eyes to widen and for him to witness his final moments. Just like his dogs, Duke Spry surrendered, showing me his metaphorical belly.

"It's you," he gasped.

But unlike with the dogs, I ripped Duke Spry's belly apart.

CHAPTER 12

I'D HOPED to walk back to the hotel under the cover of darkness, but it took a long time to find a road, and then figure out where in California I was. I eventually realized the vampire mansion had been nestled in the valleys of Mt. Tamalpais. Too far to walk without being seen. And since I was covered in blood, I couldn't hitch a ride with a good citizen without the police getting involved.

I had the duke's phone, and slumping onto a rock, I dialed Zee. He didn't answer what was an unknown number, so I left a message for him to call me back on that same number, and waited.

It rang a few minutes later.

"Ad-am? Adam . . . that you?"

"Hi Zee, yes. I'm okay." The line crackled and splintered.

". . . send . . . car . . . hear me?"

I sighed and reeled off the location a few times, hoping he could piece it together, then ended the call and settled down to watch the road.

A while later, Reynard's black sedan snaked its way up the mountain road. I wandered from the bushes and squinted at its approach, shielding my eyes. It had barely rolled to a stop when Zee flung open the back door and launched himself at me.

"Adam!" He pulled up short, cringing. "Shit, fuck, are you hurt?"

"Oh, this?" I gestured at the sticky mess of blood and bits of brain painting my clothes. "It's not mine."

"Fuck." Zee lunged, wrapped his arms around me, and crushed me close. Then his wings came in, wrapping us even tighter. "Fuck, fuck, fuck," he breathed.

"Erm. Hi."

He crushed me tighter still. "Fuck, fuck, fuck."

I choked. "Zee, easy. Kinda squishing me here," I wheezed.

"Shit." He thrust me to arms length. Emotions raced across his face—fear, rage, concern, relief. His purple eyes glistened with unshed tears. He bit into his bottom lip, to keep it from wobbling.

"Hey, I'm okay," I said. "Just messy. And tired."

"We thought . . . you were gone, and we . . . we looked. But you . . ."

I nodded and grabbed his arm, giving it a reassuring squeeze. "It's all right. Let's go home."

Reynard wasn't in the car, and Zee had to vanish his wings to fit. Even without the wings, he had to sprawl along most of the back seat, leaving one tiny little patch of leather for me to squeeze into.

"Oh, erm, it's a bit of a tight squeeze—"

He hauled me against his side, under his arm, and slotted me so close it felt as though I'd always belonged in that exact spot—like two jigsaw pieces.

The car rumbled, the wheels droned. I laid my head on his chest and listened to his heart thump. Gradually, its gallop slowed, and I fell asleep to the sound of his heart's comforting drum-like beat.

I couldn't tell him that I'd always come back to him. Always. Nothing on this earth could keep me away.

Zee must have carried me inside. I didn't remember walking through the hotel lobby. He'd probably taken me in a back door. Then, as I dozed on the bed, I listened to the sounds of a bath running. Getting clean was definitely important, but I was also kind of exhausted.

He tried to persuade me to get into the bath, but too sleepy, I refused. Then Zee was there, on the bed beside me, his arms cradling me close, his tail looped up my leg. And there, warm and safe, I slept—bloody, but not broken. I'd meant to ask after Reynard, but then I was dreaming of a big house in the clouds, encircled by a moat of blood. And inside the glowing windows, all the vampires screamed.

Steam rose off the bath, little mountains of bubbles simmered, and a squeaky duck floated at the faucet end.

"You want me to come in with you?" Zee asked, filling the entire bathroom doorway.

"In the bath?"

"Sure."

"I'm good." I smiled. "I've got this."

"I'll be right outside."

"It's okay, you know? I'm okay."

"Yeah, sure." He sniffed and shrugged like it was nothing, but his tail wrung itself behind him. "But I'll be right out here."

He closed the door, leaving it slightly ajar. I was fine with that. He clearly needed to know I was safe, and I didn't mind him peeking in.

I peeled off the stiff clothes, and grimaced. Crusty bits of gore flaked off. There was no saving that outfit. Another suit ruined.

Naked, I poked a leg through the bubbles and found the water scorching hot, then climbed in and sank below the waterline, rinsing all the chunky bits of Duke Spry from my hair.

It wasn't as though I hadn't warned him. He'd had multiple chances to let me go.

I broke the surface, gasping. Zee's face loomed an inch from mine. Big, and right there, his eyes narrowed as he studied my mouth, nose, eyes. "Oh!"

"Hey." He smiled.

"Uh . . . you okay?"

"Yes. Very okay. I'm just gonna sit right here." He flopped down against the side of the bath, draped an arm on the edge, propped his head on it, and blinked at me through the steam.

"Zee, I'm all right. I promise."

"Pfft." He rolled his eyes, and his head, making the ring in his horn glint. "I *know*."

My absence had scared him. Words alone weren't going to convince him everything was fine. I lay back in the tub and blinked at the ceiling. He could stay, I didn't mind. Liked it, in fact. It felt right having him close. Made all the jagged edges softer.

"Did they hurt you?" he mumbled, chin still resting on his arm.

"Not really." I'd hurt them, though. And vampires didn't seem the sort to let the death of a duke go unpunished.

"Good. Or I'd have to break a lot of fucking vampires in half."

Speaking of vampires—"Where's Reynard?"

"He went to negotiate with them. He's on his way back." Zee's crystalline eyes narrowed and he huffed out a great sigh. "You should know, some shit went down after you were taken."

That didn't sound good. "What shit?"

He twisted, stretched out his legs, and flopped his head back on the edge of the tub, staring at the wall. "I might have said some *things*. It was his fault you got taken, so what happened was also his fault."

Oh dear. "What did happen?"

Zee pouted. "The dance club is rubble."

I sat up, sloshing water over the sides and onto him. "Zee?"

He turned his head and lifted guilty eyes. "It's nothing, really. Just a little . . . fight." He rippled his fingers. "Reynard said he'd pay for the rebuild."

"You and Reynard fought?" It'd been brewing for a long time. Zee had already warned that only one of them would walk away from that fight. "Who won?"

He snorted. "Nobody. The furry, Abe, broke us up. It was fucking epic. Viral on socials. Reynard and me, going at it like arch-nemeses. No more fucking hashtag Reyzee. Although, there's some new shit trending." He air-quoted, "*Enemies to lovers*, whatever the fuck that is. I gotta say though, Vampire Daddy knows his moves. He got me on my back a few times, and when he wasn't trying to sink his fangs into me, it was fucking hot. But enemies to lovers? Who fucks their enemy? What kind of fucked-up romance is that?"

I smirked and lay back down in the suds. "*Now* who's into Vampire Daddy?"

He shook his head, but his little smile made a liar out of him. "Fuck that."

"Literally?"

He chuckled. "Anyway, we wrecked the club by trying to kill each other instead of going after you. Abe tried to track your scent, but the suckers took you by boat, and we lost any chance of finding you. Adam, if we hadn't—if I hadn't lost it with Reynard, we might have been able to save you. For a while, we thought . . . Shit got real, is all I'm saying. Reynard was super mad."

"It's all right," I said softly, trying to cheer him up. "I didn't need saving."

"Maybe." He mumbled. "Reynard went savage and hacked off his wife's head with her own stiletto as a new gift, or something." Zee shrugged. "Or maybe he's into skull-fucking?"

I snorted. It sounded as though I'd missed *a lot.* "I take it the baroness is dead?"

"Very." He shifted against the tub and sighed. "May I wash your back?"

I figured he needed it as much as I did. "Sure." I shifted around, so the faucets were behind me, and hugging my knees to my chest, propped my chin on them. Zee squished a sponge out, lathered it up, and swirled it over my shoulders. Soft, warm strokes kneaded tight muscles.

I flopped my head to one side and smiled through the steam, but he was taking the business of washing my back very seriously, and not looking at my face. As I watched, his wings shimmered back into the visible spectrum. They hung open and loose behind him. Relaxed. Which was good.

I hadn't meant to worry him. I'd assumed he and Reynard would think I was fine, but then, of course, they didn't have all the information. Humans generally didn't survive vampires.

The sponge roamed lower, below the waterline, down my back. I closed my eyes and a little agreeable moan slipped out from between my lips.

Zee muttered something in a language he'd never spoken around me before. Opening my eyes, I caught him watching me, and we shared a pair of soft smiles. This was nice. Really nice. Maybe a bit too nice. But he couldn't see how some parts of me were warming to his touch more than the rest.

"Turn around," he urged. "I wanna do your chest."

I wasn't going to argue, and turning back around, I leaned on the sloped part of the tub, closed my eyes, and let him massage my chest. His circular sweeps gradually worked their way lower. His hand or wrist brushed my cock, but he didn't seem to notice, and it didn't have to mean anything.

The sponge vanished, and I fluttered my eyes open to find him studying my face. His had gotten all serious.

"Want me to deal with that?" he asked, gaze flicking down.

"Only if you want," I croaked out.

"Kitten, never doubt my desire to touch your dick." He tossed the sponge and plunged his hand below the water, but I grabbed his wrist, and held it.

"I mean it," I said. "Only if you want to."

He shimmied a bit closer, and leaned in. "Any time I can touch you is a fuckin' treat. If it were up to me, I'd never let you go. And don't pull that pitying shit on me. I know my own mind, and when it comes to you, I make my own decisions. So yeah, I want to."

Freeing my hold, I dropped my head back and let my eyes fall closed. His fingers encircled my dick, giving a few warm-up strokes, hardening me off . . . and then he was all I could feel and all of the thoughts in my head. I draped my arms on the side of the tub, surrendering to him. He worked me, slow and steady . . . switched it up to fast and hard . . . then dropped off to erratic, teasing pumps, that had my balls and ass tightening. All too soon, I was ablaze. Gasping, trying not to come. Zee knew how to ride me along the edge, until I gripped the tub and pumped into his hand, chasing the fall. Ah, that's what edging was. "You *are* a master at edging." I panted, face hot and body lit up like a live wire.

"I thought I'd lost you," he growled.

I opened my eyes, and there he was, braced over me, inches from my face. Purple eyes blazed with either rage or terror—they were too similar to decipher.

"I never want to feel that again." He bared sharp teeth, adding a growl to the threat. Or was it a vow? I wasn't sure. And in a blinding surge, Zee pumped me brutally, my climax at his mercy.

I flung my head back and came so hard I saw stars. He didn't let up though, and worked my shaft through the stuttering aftershocks, wringing free every last drop.

"Kitten. You're so fucking hot when you come." His mouth brushed mine in an almost-kiss. I chased it, wanting more, wanting to drag him down into the tub with me, but he grinned and straightened, taking all of his delicious self out of reach across the bathroom.

Folding my arms on the side of the tub, I watched him saunter off—ass, tail, and wings swaying. "I don't know which is the best view," I called. "You coming, or going."

He spun, blew a kiss, and backed out of sight. "It's always coming!" he called.

I heard the main door close and sighed, all warm and fuzzy inside.

I don't deserve him.

That thought struck like an arrow to my heart. I pushed it aside, climbed from the tub and after drying off, I tucked the towel around my waist. My reflection in the dresser mirror showed no sign of my stretching the glamor. Everything was as it should be. Classic, all-American guy, who was everyone's friend and wouldn't hurt a fly. Definitely, one hundred percent human.

Zee poofed into the bedroom, behind me in the mirror, scattering sparks. He gave his wings a flick and paced. "So . . . the vampires are here."

"How many?"

He frowned, counted on his fingers, and looked up. "All of them?"

CHAPTER 13

THE ROW of black cars with little vampire monarchy flags waving on their fenders was dramatic, I'd give the vampires that. But I wasn't sure the theatrics were entirely necessary.

I shouldn't have been surprised they'd appeared on my doorstep. One of the downsides of everyone knowing you run a hotel was everyone knowing where you lived.

"You think they get a discount on black sedans?" Zee stood on the porch beside me, safely within the wards, arms folded, eyes narrowed, doing his utmost to look intimidating in high-heeled boots, creased wet shirt, and hip-clinging, frayed black pants.

I'd thrown on a sweater and slacks, leaving my hair damp. Did I look as though I'd escaped their mansion a day ago? Had it been a whole day? I'd lost track of time.

Two stoic-faced male vampires wearing identical undertaker suits approached from the second car, carrying something thin on a red cushion, as though presenting us with a gift.

"What in the actual flying fuck?" Zee muttered, spotting what was on the cushion.

The two vampires wordlessly placed the cushion and *gift* on the porch, bowed their heads, and backed up.

I blinked at the grey and shrivelled severed finger. It looked like a slug that had slithered over salt and died.

Zee shuddered. "At least it's not his dick."

Then we were both agreed, the digit probably belonged to Reynard.

I glanced over at Zee.

"I mean, I fuckin' thought there for a second, you know . . . Suckers are fucked up." He shifted uneasily, heels clicking the deck. "You lot." He flung a gesture at the vampires, encompassing the entire motorcade. "You're all psychos. A finger? What kind of mafia shit is this?"

The rest of the vampires climbed from their cars in unison, like a lineup of silent puppets, and then one on his own walked forward, climbed the steps, and flung a soggy, blood-soaked piece of paper at me. A very dead paper swan splatted on the floor.

"Meet us at midnight, at the house, Adam Vex."

"Uh, Mr. Creepy? No." Zee sassed. "Not gonna happen. Toddle your weird ass around, get back in your car, and go creep in someone else's yard."

The vampire spokesperson slid his glare to Zee, raised his top lip and spat. "*Demon spawn.*"

He turned on his heel, climbed into his car, and the procession peeled away.

"Fucking bat's balls," Zee blurted, and dropped his head back. "So much about Lord Fuck-Hard makes sense now. Can you imagine if one of them actually smiled? They'd all probably eat his heart or something. The more I meet vampires, the more I never want to fuck one."

I knelt by the cushion and poked the dried finger. "Do you think he'll want it back?"

Zee pulled a disgusted face. "I ain't touchin' it. You pick it up."

I scooped up the cushion and stood. "Aren't you supposed to put fingers on ice or something?"

He grimaced. "That appendage is beyond saving."

"We can maybe reattach it, when we get him back."

"No. Just no." He gagged, and turned away. "Take it inside."

"It's just a finger."

"Yeah but I thought it was a dick, and I can't fuckin' unsee that trauma. Fuck. *Why*?" he whined, then glanced over, reading my face. "Oh no you don't. No, you aren't saving him. This is *his* drama. Are we vampires? No. You're you, I'm me, that finger is messed up, and this is bullshit. I'm out."

Except he wasn't leaving.

"This is *his* shit," he added. "He's not our problem."

But he really was, for multiple reasons. "Zee. Reynard's name is in the guest book. He's a guest. That means he's under my protection—*our* protection. And I . . . kind of . . . like him. A little bit."

Zee stared at the porch ceiling for a few seconds, smiled in resignation, and closed his eyes. "Right. Fine. Okay. Fuck." He gave his wings a flick, and muttered about saving skinny vampires not being in his contract. "Wait here, I'm going to get changed. And before you argue, I'm coming with you— no discussion."

"Okay, just . . . What are you going to wear? Because there were some things in your wardrobe that might not be appropriate for, erm, a high-stakes meeting with vampire royalty."

"Are you talking about the sub outfit, with the—" He gestured at his crotch. His eyes lit up, ideas sparking. "Fuck, that would give those suckers something to swoon over. My cock in a leather sling. Can you imagine their faces?"

"Unfortunately, yes."

"Says you, standing there with a shriveled finger on a cushion like a weird-ass Cinderella's prince." He grinned, flicked his fingers, and vanished. I had no idea if he'd be wrapped in leather ties when I next saw him. But in the meantime, I did have a finger to store somewhere safe.

If I was going back to Vampire Mansion, where they'd likely be a little bit irritated by the mess I'd left behind, I needed more help than one horny demon wearing a cock sling. For what happened next, I needed to pay Tom Collins a visit.

With the finger stowed away on ice—and after I'd avoided Tom Collins's attempt to fill me full of alcohol—I returned to the lobby, and heard a tittering commotion bubbling outside. *What now?* A few smiling, chatting guests pushed through the door, and I caught a glimpse of a demon on the porch. My demon, but . . . not. Catching the door before it swung shut, I gaped at the stunning warrior posing for selfies on the steps, where phones had a better chance of working.

Leather armor clung to Zee's outline, from his collar to his studded riding boots.

He posed with a vicious looking curved sword, leaning on it like a cane. Then he kicked it up, spun it flawlessly, and struck a *"grrr"* pose, much to the delight of the filming guests.

They probably thought his outfit was some kind of prop, or cosplay, but that sword was real.

And so was his armor.

He was *magnificent*.

Zee saw me, and shooed the guests away. He preened, eyebrows bouncing. "Not just a demon who sucks cock for cash. And if you tell anyone this getup is real, I'll laugh you off as insane."

"I wouldn't dream of it." I descended the few steps and reached out to stroke over his leather-clad arm. Buckles glistened here and there. The craftsmanship was a work of art. His wings sprouted through special slots in the back, and their tips glistened with metallic points.

The armor had been lovingly custom made *for* him.

I circled him, stroking over perfectly stitched seams, and made it back around to his front.

"Keep looking at me like that and I'll get hard—not fun in tight leather."

"You're stunning, Zee."

He bowed. "Why, thank you, kind sir." Rising, he fluttered his fingers at me. "You're making me look overdressed. Where's your armor?"

I tugged at my yellow sweater. "This is my armor."

"Oh Adam, my sweet, dull-as-dishwater kitten. You're walking into a mansion brimming with humorless vampires looking like a sunshine twink?"

That was precisely what I was doing. I smiled. "I'll do the talking, you do the fighting. You ready?"

"I was fuckin' born ready." He sheathed the sword at his hip. "Let's go fuck up some vampires."

Zee used his phone to summon Reynard's driver, and we both clambered into the back of the car—not an easy task with all Zee's spikey bits.

"It wasn't made for confined spaces." He wriggled, yanking at his crotch. Leather squeaked on leather, and creaked every time the car rumbled over a bump.

"You could fly there?" I suggested, after suffering a few bumped elbows.

"And get shot at by every gun-happy demon hater? I'm good, thanks."

My sweater snagged on one of his chest buckles. "We're uh . . ."

"Don't pull on it, it'll unravel."

"I just—" I tried to unhook it, he leaned in, the car jolted over a bump, his horns hit the roof lining, and my sweater frayed when the loose thread opened a little hole. Our gazes met, and we both laughed. Despite the circumstances, this was almost fun.

I laid my hand on his chest, and he pried the thread off the buckle, freeing me, but I stayed close and peered up at him. Who was he really, in his past life beyond the veil? Someone important among demons? Someone dangerous? Someone worthy of the sword he carried and the armor he wore? Not that he wasn't worthy as Zee the porn star, just . . . different.

"So . . ." he puffed. "This is a lot of fuss, just so a random baron can gift a nobody hotelier to their queen, right? Are vamps always this overdramatic and twitchy?"

I sat back and avoided his gaze. "I may have accidentally kicked a hornets' nest."

"Adam, what did you do?"

"I mean . . . They were rude, so . . ." I clasped my knees and shrugged. "It's just a little thing."

"Oh. Okay. Just a little thing. Which is why they sent us Lord Reynard's finger on a cushion?"

"Look, I don't know, I just . . . I escaped. And maybe some vampires might have died at the same time, which had absolutely nothing to do with me at all."

"So, they randomly dropped dead, because immortal assholes are totally known for just up and dying?"

That was a thing that happened sometimes. "Exactly."

"Who died?"

"Dunno."

He huffed a chuckle. "You're so cute when you lie. Was it someone important?"

"Maybe."

He dropped his head back, but rolled his eyes toward me

and jumped his eyebrows. "It's a good thing I have a big sword."

A little while later, our driver pulled up outside a pair of huge gates topped with stone gargoyles, who may or may not be actual gargoyles. Zee and I hopped out, and sauntered up the gravel track toward a second pair of gates—these ones closed—and a guard house.

The vampire behind the reinforced glass eyed the pair of us and frowned.

"Hello. I'm Adam Vex, and this is my business partner, Zodiac—"

"I know who you are. Sign here." He shoved a clipboard through the slot. We scribbled our signatures, and the guard took the clipboard back. He opened a hatch and shoved a black tray at us. "Leave your weapons."

"We're not carrying any weapons," Zee said with a straight face, while dressed like one enormous metal-tipped murder machine.

"Demon, are you really going to pretend you do not have a scimitar sheathed at your hip?" the guard drawled, sighing.

"Oh, this old thing?" Zee shrugged. "It's barely even sharp."

"Put the sword in the tray."

Zee huffed, and stalled, eyeing the enormous mansion with its bajillion windows. "You've got, what . . . a hundred vampires in there? Are all your dicks so small one little demon with a blunt sword is a threat?"

The guard's eyes narrowed. "Whatever. You?" he asked me.

"I'm just a human."

He punched the gate button, and the rows of huge, ornate iron bars rumbled open.

"Clearly, he loves his job," I muttered to Zee as we passed

through, back into the grounds of the house I'd fled all too recently.

"Remind me again why I'm walking into vampire central with one fucking sword and a cute human?" Zee asked from the corner of his mouth.

"To get Reynard back."

"Ugh. He owes me after this."

"This'll be good for us. Like a trust exercise."

"Trust exercise? Such as when you close your eyes and fall back into your partner's arms—that kind of trust exercise?"

"Yes, exactly."

"Kitten, this is not some team-building, touch-feely shit. This is a survival of the fittest exercise. This is a fuck-them-up-before-they-fuck-us-up exercise. Just know, nobody is getting anywhere near you unless they want fifty inches of Damascus steel shoved up their ass."

"You don't need to worry. I've got this." I beamed.

He blinked. "Oh, okay. That's fine then. So you have a plan? It had better be a fucking amazing plan, because I'm sensing more than a few suckers in this house, and most of them are sexually repressed and grumpy. When we walk through those doors, we will be vastly outnumbered. So what's this great plan?"

"We're going to parley."

"Talking is your plan?"

"I told you it was."

"Talking?" He laughed. "Alright, fine. But if that doesn't work, can I slaughter them?"

It wouldn't come to that. "No killing. We don't want to make this worse."

Zee rolled his eyes, horns, and head. "Maiming, then? Just a little stabby stabby with my sword, and oops, there goes an arm?"

"Maiming is okay, I guess."

"Awesome." He skipped a step. "It's been a long while since Shareen tasted vampire blood."

"Shareen?"

He patted the sword's handle sticking up from his hip. "My sword."

"You've killed vampires before?" I whispered, keeping my voice down as we approached the main steps.

He shrugged his wings. "A few."

Zee said *"a few,"* the way I claimed I was one hundred percent human.

The mansion's huge front doors yawned open, revealing a single vampire footman. "Good evening, right this way please." Enormous portraits of severe looking vampires watched our passing, like gods peering down at ants.

"Tea?" the footman asked, after he'd escorted us to some kind of reception room with a roaring fireplace and cute, mismatched furniture.

"Erm, no thank you."

"Wait here a moment." He left, gently clicking the door closed, sealing us in a silence broken only by the crackling fire.

"Is it creepy how they all look the same? It's creepy right?" Zee muttered, wandering the room and poking at ornaments. "Like copy and paste vampires." He mumbled on, examining weird little porcelain dolls spread about on the occasional tables. "There are way too many trinkets in here."

Those in the cars, the guard in the guardhouse, even the footman—they'd all resembled each other. Not exact copies, but definitely lookalikes. "Like drones."

"If Ted Bundy had a mansion, this would be it. Is Bundy a vampire?" Zee picked up a porcelain cat from the mantle-piece. "Hey, lo—"

"Right this way," the footman announced, appearing suddenly inside the door.

Zee spun. "Fuck!" His tail sideswiped one of the many delicate ornaments, like a bat strikes a ball, and the thing hurtled across the room. It punched through a window and was gone, sailing into the night.

A few, tense seconds ticked by.

The footman cleared his throat. "As I was saying, right this way, please."

"I'll uh . . . pay for that." Zee strutted forward.

"Very well," the footman drawled, eying Zee down his nose as he passed by him through the door.

This was going well. I followed Zee, my back tingling under the footman's glare. We passed through the reception hall, into a back corridor, down a few steps, and finally—when it seemed as though we'd been walking in circles—the footman pushed open double doors into an enormous ballroom, lined with floor-standing candelabra and draped in dramatic shadows.

"Mr. Adam Vex, and his demon," the footman announced, for the benefit of the four vampires seated in high-backed chairs on a raised stage area. One chair was empty.

"This is very *Anne Rice*," Zee remarked, teeth glinting.

In front of the vampires, on his knees, hands bound behind his back and splattered with blood, knelt Reynard.

I'd seen him comatose on his bedroom floor, but this was worse, because he was conscious. He panted through gritted teeth. His hair was a ragged mess, curtained around his face. Blood pooled under him, which didn't seem like a good thing since vampires generally liked blood on the inside. But worse, his anguish crackled like electricity before a lightning strike.

He was furious—and petrified.

"Fuck me," Zee whispered, his smile long gone. Even he didn't want to see Reynard like this. He could probably sense his emotions, too, better than I could.

Daisy, the eleven-year-old mystery girl the duke had

bowed to, pushed from her throne. All the chairs were clearly thrones, I noted, as we approached the stage. She approached Reynard—ponytail swishing—planted a hand on her hip, and waited as we walked the last few meters down the long, empty room.

"Demon. Curtail your foul tongue in this house," one of the male vampires ordered.

"Suck my dick, vampire."

The vampire growled, and tensed in his posh chair.

"Enough," Daisy snapped, then settled her glare on me. "Hello again, Mr. Vex. Please silence your demon so we can chat like grown-ups."

This looking down on demons as though they were lesser creatures was getting tiresome. "If you'd like Zee to be quiet, ask him nicely."

Zee's wings ruffled. "Yeah, Buffy." A broad grin swept across his face, revealing rows of sharp teeth. "Ask me nicely."

Daisy slow-blinked—like I'd seen Reynard do—buying herself several seconds of thinking time. "Lycian, Scourge of Demios, Butcher of Knowles," she said, addressing . . . Zee?

Zee shrugged. "No idea, but he sounds fucking hot."

"I ask you to refrain from using foul language while we discuss this reprobate." She kicked Reynard so hard he grunted and slumped lower, almost kissing the stage.

Zee's tail lashed. "I'll refrain from fucking foul language if you refrain from kicking him."

Daisy crouched, and cradled Reynard's chin in her hand, lifting his pale face. "Hm, it almost sounds as though you care, demon. Which cannot be. No member of my family would ever debase themselves with a demon. If I discovered such a foul union, I'd tear out the baron's heart and crush it."

All this racist posturing was beginning to grate. "Victor Reynard is under our protection as a guest of the SOS Hotel,"

I announced. "While he remains a guest, you have no claim over him."

Daisy frowned, jerked Reynard's head away and jolted to her feet. "What nonsense is this?" She turned to her retinue. "Pierce, what is he referring to?"

"Nothing, my liege. Although . . . it does sound as though he might have a minor claim, if this guest book is legitimate—"

"It's not nothing," I said, louder. "His name is in the guest book. The hotel guest book is a type of contract. Which means Reynard is *mine*." A silence rushed in, so thick it was almost preternatural. "I mean . . . he's free to choose . . . to be mine. He has my protection, the same as every other guest in my hotel does." Had I salvaged that?

Even Reynard turned his head, and eyed me with a blood-shot glare. I couldn't tell if he cared at all about my claim to protect him, but he wasn't panting as fast as he had been.

"Yours?" Daisy scoffed. "And who are you, exactly, Adam Vex? Because all of us here are confused, as to how or why an apparent human—wearing enormously powerful glamor—is playing hard and fast with Lost Ones' vows and rules, as though you're not just a human, but something far more attuned to how the world works." Daisy approached the edge of the stage. "You stand there, with a serial killer at your side, claiming my baron is under your protection, and you expect us to believe you're just a human? Not to mention the fact you killed four ward weavers, and *my duke!*" She yelled the last part.

Also, Zee was a serial killer?

He shrugged, acting like he had no clue what Daisy was referring to. We could come back to that later.

I sighed. "I don't know anything about any of what you just said—"

"Liar! Where's my duke?" Daisy stamped her foot.

"I don't know." Bits of him had been stuck in my hair, but I doubted she'd react well to that fact. The rest of him . . . well, it wasn't ever going to be found.

"He was last seen tracking *you*, Adam Vex. What did you do to him?"

"Maybe he's still out there? There's a lot of forest to get lost in."

She glared, fists pinned to her sides. "Where's his body?"

"See, if you don't have a body, then he's clearly still alive."

"You killed a guard in your escape—crushed his skull— Duke Spry was sent to retrieve you, and he has not been seen since. Do you think I'm an idiot, Mr. Vex?"

"Maybe you shouldn't have taken Adam then?" Zee suggested. "Did you bite off more than you can chew, girly?"

"The very fact you're standing in my house is an insult to my entire family. My mommy will be *displeased*. You do not want her to be displeased, demon."

"Enough," I grumbled. "Hand Victor over and we're even. Nobody else needs to get hurt."

"Even?" She coughed a laugh. "We'll never be even! You killed Uncle Spry!"

Zee rolled his eyes. "You don't have a dead body, cupcake. No body, no murder. You got Baroness Reynard's head. If your uncle is anything like the rest of you psychos, he's probably a kiddie-fiddler. This whole shit-show is done. Reynard is ours, so back the fuck off."

"Oh, we're a long way from done. No demon or human can tell me what to do. I'm the princess. Mommy is the queen. And you're both *fucking dead!"*

CHAPTER 14

DAISY LUNGED off the stage at me, fingers spread like talons and fangs bared. I dodged right. Zee intercepted, sword flashing, and Daisy let out a cry. Reynard's growl rumbled like thunder, and it was around then I figured talks had broken down enough to whip out my secret weapon.

I gave Gideon's signet ring—which I'd gotten off Tom Collins—a half turn, and said, "*Shadow*."

Technically, they didn't have to come. I wasn't a sorcerer and hadn't bound them. But I had asked them nicely, and since they'd been staying in our attic and gorging themselves on gremlins, who knew? They'd agreed.

All the shadows in the room surged, hundreds of candles spluttered, and a menacing roar erupted. The ambient light drowned under Shadow's sweeping arrival, but I saw flashes among the chaos—Zee with his sword raised, vampires flung by Shadow's sweeping arms.

I stumbled to the stage, climbed up, and found Reynard frantically writhing against his restraints.

"Unbind me, Adam!" He seethed, teeth snapping. *"I will slay them all."*

I laid a hand on his shoulder and leaned in, shutting out the sounds of screams and the wet splatter of steel cutting through flesh. "Victor, look at me." He blinked wild eyes, but gradually stopped bucking. "You're not thinking clearly. If you fight them, you will die, and I don't want that to happen."

"Adam?" He panted. "They hurt you. *They will pay in blood!*"

"No, no blood." I needed him back in the room, not lost to his murderous impulses. "I'm alright." I snapped his ties, hoping that later he didn't remember how easily I'd freed him, and placed his trembling hand over my heart. "See? I'm fine. You know what will hurt me more? Seeing you hurt. I just want to go home. With you. And Zee."

Reynard's head twitched. He looked behind me, silver eyes widening. Images danced in his eyes, of a demon warrior cutting down vampires. "Zodiac," he whispered. "He fights for me?"

"For *us.*"

I needed to get them both home before this brawl escalated. There were a lot more vampires in the house who had yet to arrive.

Scooping Reynard against me, we hobbled off the stage, and headed for the door at the far end of the long hall. The shadows still danced, swirling around the room. Steel struck steel. Vampires hissed. If Zee wasn't by the door, I'd return for him. I just had to get Reynard out.

We made it out the door, and Zee plunged from the ceiling, dashing through behind us. He grabbed a nearby candelabra, knocked the candles off, rammed it through the door handles, and bent it in a knot, sealing the vampires inside with Shadow.

We hurried back out of the house, across the grounds, and

the bored, inept guard buzzed us through the gate without looking up.

Reynard's driver spotted us, spun the wheels, surged up to the driveway, and screeched the car to a halt. I manhandled Reynard into the rear seat, then stuck my leg in, about to climb in—but there was no chance Zee would fit.

"You go. I'll fly," he said, backing up.

"But you'll get shot at."

"I'll fly high. It's just cold. I got this. And I can make sure you're not followed, from above. Go."

"Thanks, Zee."

He snorted. "Best fucking night out I've had in forever. Go home, *both* of you. I'll meet you there." He thumped the car roof, spread his wings, and shot skyward, as sleek and fast as an arrow.

I watched him vanish among the stars, then climbed in next to Reynard. The driver sped us away from the house as soon as I'd gotten the door closed. After we'd traveled a few miles, I twisted the ring, sending a message to Shadow to stand down. Whether they did or not was up to them.

"Adam," Reynard croaked.

"Hey." Shuffling closer, along the seat, I hoped my smile eased some of the pain he had to be suffering. "Do you need blood?"

His throat moved as he dry swallowed, and those eyes already said sorry for what came next. I didn't mind, I healed more quickly than he realized.

"There's a supply in the chiller," the driver said.

"Oh." That made things less awkward. A little button opened a storage compartment under the seats, and from there, I removed the unmarked bottle.

Reynard snatched it, tore the lid off, and gulped it as fast as an alcoholic determined to drown at the bottom. Done, he slumped back and let the bottle fall from his hand. Under the soft glow of the car's lighting, I watched all the bloody cuts and grazes stitch themselves closed one by one. From his tight face and gritted teeth, I figured it was pretty painful.

"If only the cuts on the inside healed as easily."

"Adam," he croaked again. "Where do I begin repaying you? How can I make this right? I never intended for any of this—"

"Well, that's a lie, but I accept you didn't know what you were agreeing to in trading me as a gift. Perhaps you'll refrain from gifting human beings in future?"

His fine, dark eyes had no business being so soft and sorrow filled. "Can you find it in your heart to forgive me?"

The way he asked made me want to climb into his lap, take his face in my hands, and kiss him breathless. "Thank Zee, and I'll consider it."

"I will." His hand found mine and clamped on, *hard,* as we both pretended none of this was anything more than a business arrangement. I'd told myself so many lies over the years, what was another little one?

The car cruised across the Golden Gate Bridge, its strings of lights sparkling like artificial stars. "I fear this is not over," Reynard said.

No, it wasn't over. But at least the San Franciscan vampires knew I wasn't the easy prey they'd mistaken me for. They'd think twice about coming for me and mine in the future. Because, make no mistake, Reynard *was* mine. And so was Zee.

My heart twisted.

They were mine, but neither of them knew what that meant. They had a right to know . . .

"Adam?"

"Hm?" Dragging my gaze inside the car, I caught his concerned expression. "Oh, it's nothing. Just tired. It's been a tough few days."

"*Did* you slay the duke?" he asked.

I pressed my lips together and turned my face away, but Reynard's reflection floating in the black glass saw my guarded expression.

The metaphorical cage bars had begun to shrink around me again. Any tighter, and I'd suffocate. The SOS Hotel was not supposed to be a prison. And it never would be. Not for a single name in the book.

But my name wasn't in there.

Because Adam Vex was a mask I wore, no more real than the glamor wrapped around me.

CHAPTER 15

AFTER SWITCHING out the signet ring for Reynard's finger, I left Reynard in his room to lick his wounds—literally! Ick—and returned to the bar to find Zee already on a stool. He'd ditched the leathers for a handsome purple and black kilt, black boots, and purple vest.

It must have been late, or early, because we were the only ones in the bar, and the hotel had that soft, sleeping vibe. The old building was snoozing too. The jukebox played some tinkling, upbeat jazz.

Tom Collins poured me a whiskey. Zee already had a fancy cocktail in a curvy glass, and together, we sat in silence, mulling over the past few days.

A lot had happened.

Reynard's wife, the plot to kill her, some wild sex on the roof that may or may not have boosted the hotel wards, a very dead duke, and a pissed off vampire princess.

"Serial killer, huh?" I said.

He tried to smile and almost made it stick. "Warrior is the technical term, but suckers are *so* dramatic." He rolled his eyes, like he didn't thrive on drama.

"And this *Lycian* person?"

He picked up his drink and sipped the glittery concoction. "He doesn't exist here."

We all had parts of ourselves we hid from others. I understood what it meant to forget the past in order to survive the future, more than he could ever know. "Besides helping me get Reynard back?"

"Fuck off! Me help a vampire?" He snorted. "Never happened." But he smiled as he spoke, so it wasn't all bad. "How is Vampire Daddy?"

"Did you know vampire saliva has healing properties? No, I didn't either, until he sucked on his finger and reattached it."

He gagged and shoved his palm in my face. "Don't. I can't. So nasty." He downed his sparkly cocktail, and waggled the empty glass for Tom Collins to refill. "Hey, Tom Collins, hit me with your class A cocktails. I need to get so wasted I forget the past forty-eight hours ever happened."

"You're the boss, boss." Tom Collins saluted, then tossed a bunch of brightly colored drinks together, shook them up, added some spinning mixers and fancy moves—and some white dust from a tiny bag—then presented it to Zee with a flourish.

Zee took a sip of the purple cocktail. "That's a kick. If you weren't an AI, I'd fuck you. Although, you must have a socket, right?"

"You're welcome, Zodiac. No physical fucking required. Your handsome smile is enough. And payment before you leave."

I chuckled as Tom sauntered to the other end of the bar.

"He's kinda hot," Zee remarked, watching Tom Collins's virtual ass. "You think he's hot?"

"You think *everything* is hot."

"If he's real enough to hold a glass, he's real enough to

hold other things, right?" Zee grinned. "Do you think he has a dick? Did they program that in? What else did they program?" His eyes widened. "I've never fucked an AI."

I laughed at his verbal train of thought. "Please don't break the AI more than he already is."

"Pfft." He huffed a little laugh, and we fell into a comfortable silence, until he said, "We made some enemies tonight, Adam."

"We did," I agreed. There was no denying it. Daisy was not likely to forget the death of her Uncle Spry. And if *she* was bad, then her mother was likely a hundred times scarier. "But they learned we're no pushover."

The bar door creaked, and Lord Reynard strode in. His pinstripe shirt hung untucked over black pants—the most badly creased clothing I'd ever seen him wear. He'd plaited his hair in a messy braid, and looked a thousand times hotter —slightly disheveled and a tiny bit unhinged—than when he was made of perfect lines.

He sat to my right. "Tea, please."

"Tea?" Tom Collins's bartender feelings shriveled in his programming.

"Fine," Reynard nodded. "Add a dash of something potent."

Tom Collins whipped out a tea cup and pot from somewhere under the bar, suggesting Reynard's tea was a regular ask. "For a second there, Victor," Tom began. "I thought you and I were going to have a fucking disagreement."

We waited, while Tom prepared the tea, enjoying the clink of the spoon on the fine china cup, and the slosh of hot water. With Zee to my left, I expected the usual tension to start fizzing the wards, charging them, should they need to kick in and slap either of them down. But they hadn't yet triggered.

"Vampire," Zee grumbled.

"Demon."

I blinked. After everything we'd been through, they could extend the courtesy of addressing each other properly. "How about we all use our names like grown-ups?"

"Which name?" Zee asked. "I've got a few for Fuck-Hard. Some might even get his blood fired up."

"What did you call me?" Reynard's metaphorical hackles rose, and the wards simmered.

I slapped my hands on the bar. "Stop."

They both glowered, but soon wilted under my alternating scowl.

"Victor," I said. "You have something to say to Zee?" I'd used his first name out of respect, but also to show we'd gone beyond mere acquaintances. In truth, I had no idea what he and I were.

Reynard breathed in, lifting his shoulders. He turned his head, then twisted on the stool to present Zee with his full attention. Leaning back, out of the way, I gave them both room.

"Zodiac. Thank you for coming to my aid. I am in your debt." He bowed his head.

I looked at Zee, waiting for his response. He sat very still —even his tail had frozen—then he huffed, unlocking himself. "No idea what you're talking about. Never happened."

"As you wish," Reynard conceded, and they both went back to their drinks.

Was that progress? It felt like a tiny step in the right direction, but we were still a long way from group hugs.

"I can't ever go back," Reynard said, after we'd all stewed in a few minutes of quiet contemplation.

"It won't be a finger next time," Zee said, agreeing.

"I know that, de— Zodiac." Reynard snarled, then caught my narrowed eyes and sighed. "As a widow, they'll demand I remarry, or die. I'd rather die than be chained to someone I despise. There is no direction to turn in which I am free."

Clearly, he needed to have more faith in me and the hotel. "There won't be a next time, Victor. Family is not blood, it's who you choose. For as long as your name is in the book, you're welcome here. And safe."

"Thank you."

Two little words—thank you—but the emotion in his eyes showed how he truly meant them. I knew what it was to be driven from your home, to lose everything you thought you'd loved, to be alone.

"They're fucking psycho suckers anyway," Zee said. "Why would you want to go back, when you've got the best fucking bartender in the city right here, music to suit your mood, Adam, who is frankly the best, and a whole selection of guests to feast on—"

"No, we don't do that." I cut him off. "Do we, Zee?"

"Nooooo, we definitely *do not do that*." His eyes got all big, like a cat about to pounce, and his lashes fluttered. "I was thinking of that *other* hotel. Shithole. Full of gremlins. Nobody wants to stay *there*."

"Thank you, Adam. Truly," Reynard said, his lips hinting at a smile, as though maybe Zee's humor had chipped off some of his icy vampire armor, thawing him out.

"We're all orphans, right?" Both of their stares snapped to me. Oops. "I mean, *you're* all orphans. The Lost Ones, that is —not me. Ha ha. Someone has to look after you. If it's not me, who will?! Anyhoo . . ." I hopped off the stool. "Good night." The combined weight of their gazes followed me out the door.

Hopefully, I'd salvaged that mishap.

Of course, neither were fools, and if they'd been paying attention, there were a great many things about me—average human, Adam Vex—that didn't add up. The vampires knew it now too. And they were up to something . . . I'd only gotten a glimpse of their operation, but it seemed clear they'd been preparing for *an event,* like the arrival of their queen. A queen who wasn't supposed to be here. Did they have a means of opening the veil? And if they did, did that mean the Lost Ones could go home?

I shuddered at the thought.

It wasn't any of my business.

I'd already made too many waves.

In two weeks, I'd made an enemy of a sorcerer who knew I had secrets, and now I'd managed to enrage the entire San Franciscan vampire hierarchy. But it wasn't all bad. I'd made friends with a shadowbeast—and kinda adopted a vampire daddy with benefits, and a demon who didn't just suck cock for cash but could wield a sword like a badass.

Hopefully, the SOS Hotel had reached peak drama, and the next few weeks would be boring, in a good way.

The sound of tires screeching drew my eye toward the hotel's front doors.

I pushed through, onto the front porch, and breathed in San Francisco's fresh early-morning air. A few stars twinkled in the distance, but the red morning sky had begun to threaten, chasing them into oblivion.

A mound of discarded trash bags lay by the side of the steps. That wasn't right. It wasn't trash collection day until the end of the week. I sauntered down the steps. The wards sizzled, warning me I was nearing their new, extended edge.

The trash bags weren't trash bags.

My breath caught.

A demon, wrapped in a pink and black polyester outfit lay face down in the flowerbeds, her wings bent at painful angles.

My heart lurched. I dashed to her side, and rolled her over. Empty, pale pink eyes stared through me, with no life left in them.

"Oh no."

A magenta enveloped was taped to her chest. The three words scrawled in messy, jagged writing on the front, read:

Stoopid Letle Homan

I picked up the envelope, and flicked it open, unleashing a whiff of musky, masculine cologne.

U had fun

No maw gamz

Zee iz mine, betch

Seb

He'd signed off with a heart. The message was clear. Sebastien wanted Zee back, and he'd kill to get him.

I stuffed the envelope into my pocket and sighed at the unfortunate demon.

If Zodiac knew demons were dying because of him, he'd go back to Seb in a heartbeat.

I swept a hand down the demon's face, closing her eyes.

No body, meant no murder.

The street was empty. A few remaining stars fought the dawn above, my only witnesses. And I knew what I had to do.

To be continued . . .

COMING UP IN SOS HOTEL #3

Zee grunted. "Deeper."

"I am."

"Shove it in harder."

"It's too small."

"Kitten, have you seen the size of the hole? Put some hip action into it." He huffed, bent over the rickety cabinet, hugging all the panels in place with his arms and tail. "Did you lube?"

I was trying to manhandle the cabinet's side panel into its longer back panel, lining up the little wooden-dowel things with their holes. But it wasn't going so well. Although, from the tittering snickers among customers in the bar, they appeared to be enjoying the show.

"I don't have any lube," I told Zee.

"I can't hold it. Thrust, Adam."

"I am thrusting!" I jerked my hips, trying to pump the panel into place.

"May I be of assistance?" Lord Reynard chose that precise moment to appear in the corner of my vision. I puffed my bangs from my sticky face, while awkwardly contorted around the end of the cabinet. Reynard stood back, eyebrow arched in silent judgment, holding the instruction pamphlet I hadn't read. And neither had Zee.

"Does it look like we need *your* help?" Zee grumbled. "Hold it!"

Reynard's beautiful, dark-lined silvery eyes swiveled to Zee, then cut back to me, querying whether we wanted an answer.

Of course he'd had to appear while I had my ass in the air and appeared to be humping a poorly put together piece of furniture. "Uh, I think we're—" My grip on the panel slipped and the rickety cabinet buckled. Its doors popped off, the legs twanged, and drawer shot up toward my face. Reynard grabbed my shoulder, and spun me into his firm arms as though we were back on the dance floor, just in time for me to watch Zee sprawl onto the floor with the cabinet.

He sprang back to his feet, flared his wings, and hissed at the now flattened piece of furniture. "No. I am done. You need eight arms to put this shit together. It's like fucking Jenga."

"In Jenga, don't you take pieces out?" I asked.

"Huh?" Zee grunted.

"Did you read the instructions?" Reynard asked, his warm arm still tucked around me.

"Did I read the—pfft." Zee barked a laugh. "*Did I read the instructions?*" he mocked, in Reynard's accent. "Instructions are for losers and control freaks. Oh, and there I see you're holding them. *And* Adam. There's a surprise. Also, those instructions are in Swedish. You fucking read Swedish, Your Highness?"

Oh dear.

"I do," Reynard replied calmly. "And please, I'm a mere

baron. Your Highness is reserved for the immediate royal family."

Zee's tail rattled and his eyes narrowed to dagger-like slits. But the wards didn't tingle, so that was good, right?

If I'd expected them to get along since we'd plucked Reynard out of his family's clutches, I'd clearly been a bit too optimistic.

Zee picked up a hammer, took a single step closer, and dropped the hammer at Reynard's feet with a heavy clang. "Have at it, Fancy Daddy." He flicked his horns and strutted off, hips rocking, boots punctuating the floor.

"Why does he insist on referring to me as his father when we are clearly not related?"

"Oh, uh, I have no idea." I extracted myself from the comfortable niche under Reynard's arm, and brushed sawdust from my clothes and ruffled hair. The cabinet had beaten Zee and me, but making flatpack furniture had never been my forte, and Zee definitely wasn't going to give it another shot with Reynard overseeing him.

"Why don't you take a break and I'll see what I can do?" Reynard asked. He shrugged off his jacket and draped it over a nearby chair, then folded his shirt sleeves up.

I could have watched Reynard's precise fingers tease those shirt cuffs all day. He made each gesture precise, each pinch of those fingers had its place, and every little fold over was performed with perfect accuracy, ensuring no gesture was wasted.

Catching myself staring, I cleared my throat. "Are you sure? Don't you have better things to be doing?"

"I have some time. The company largely runs itself." He picked up the instructions and leafed through them. "This shouldn't take long."

If he made that cabinet as perfect as he had made the

paper swan he'd once given me, Zee would despise it. "Erm . . . Maybe don't make it too perfect?"

He looked up and grimaced, as though I'd suggested he roll in mud. "You're asking me to *fail*?"

"Not fail, exactly. Just . . . you know . . ." How was I supposed to ask him to half-ass it so Zee didn't have yet another thing to gripe about.

"No, I don't know. Explain, Adam. A job worth doing is worth doing properly. Why would I sabotage my own efforts?"

Ugh. Vampires. I sighed and glanced across the bar, checking Zee hadn't returned and wasn't within listening distance. "Just trust me. It'll make our lives easier if you're less than perfect."

"Well, that is a tall order." His mouth ticked at one corner. "But I will try and oblige."

"Good, that's good. I'll uh . . . go get cleaned up . . ."

He bowed his head and turned, to begin assembling the cabinet. I'd have liked to have watched, but unlike his company, the SOS Hotel did not run itself, and required constant attention so it didn't collapse like a house of cards around me. At least the work kept me busy, and my mind off *other* things. I pushed through the bar door, into the lobby, and found Zee standing with a single-horned demon at one of the waiting-area tables. As I moved around, I recognized Ramone—the demon from Razorsedge who had helped us dispatch Reynard's wife.

He raised his hand and threw me a smile. He was shorter than Zee by several feet, but stockier, and packed with more muscle under his plain clothing.

I made my way over, but Ramone's smile faded fast the nearer I got. This couldn't be good.

"Adam," Ramone said. "I hope you don't mind me coming here?"

"Not at all. You're welcome any time."

Zee perched his ass on the arm of the tired chair. His wings drooped, and his tail lay limp on the floor. I didn't need to look at his face to know what I'd see there. Something bad had happened.

To be continued . . .

ABOUT THE AUTHOR

Zee: *Adam is too humble to write anything here, and if Reynard attempts it, we'll all die of boredom. So, you lovely people, have the honor of my glorious company. I'm going to tell you the story of Adam Vex. Gather 'round, here goes…*

Once upon a time, a human was born (Do not recommend watching. Very slimy. Not fun). His name was Adam. He survived despite being a soft, squishy manbaby, until he was 24 years old. One night, he ~~found~~ saved a demon (me) and for some fucking reason I still haven't figured out, he wanted my help to buy and run a forgotten hotel. Most everyone thought he was crazy. He probably is.

Turns out, he's not as squishy as most humans, but we don't talk about that.

He does have a soft heart, and if anyone hurts him, I will pull their fucking limbs off and beat them to death with their own arms.

He likes cats. His favorite color is brown. And sometimes, when I look at him, and he doesn't know, he seems sad. The kind of sad that touches your insides. But when he sees me, and smiles, the sadness vanishes. It's still there, though. Hidden.

I like it best when he smiles. His smile warms me through like sunshine on my wings.

But this page ain't about me, it's about Adam Vex, the best fucking human in all of San Francisco. He's awesome. He saved me, bought a hotel, and now he kinda wants to save everyone else too…

SOS HOTEL
FOR A SUPERNATURALLY SAFE STAY!
Lord Reynard won't be staying
WTF?!
MM becomes MMM
AN MM URBAN FANTASY
Adam Vex
SOS HOTEL
FOR A SUPERNATURALLY SAFE STAY!
#1
Adam Vex
SOS HOTEL
#2
me!
ex porn star demon
the REAL star!
Free gremlins
dark
the way u like it
definitely 100% normal human
not sus
fun shit
Explicit
sex, drugs, booze
all the fucks
SOME minor murders
he's the best
Adam Vex
ARIANA NASH WRITING AS
Zodiac

Printed in Great Britain
by Amazon